By Philip Roth

DECEPTION

THE FACTS

THE COUNTERLIFE

ZUCKERMAN BOUND

THE ANATOMY LESSON

ZUCKERMAN UNBOUND

A PHILIP ROTH READER

THE GHOST WRITER

THE PROFESSOR OF DESIRE

READING MYSELF AND OTHERS

MY LIFE AS A MAN

THE GREAT AMERICAN NOVEL

THE BREAST

OUR GANG

PORTNOY'S COMPLAINT

WHEN SHE WAS GOOD

LETTING GO

GOODBYE, COLUMBUS

DECEPTION

a novel by

PHILIP ROTH

SIMON AND SCHUSTER

New York London Toronto Sydney Tokyo Singapore

SIMON AND SCHUSTER
Simon & Schuster Building
Rockefeller Center
1230 Avenue of the Americas
New York, New York 10020

SIMON AND SCHUSTER and colophon are registered
trademarks of Simon & Schuster Inc.

Designed by Laurie Jewell
Manufactured in the United States of America

1   3   5   7   9   10   8   6   4   2

Library of Congress Cataloging in Publication Data
Roth, Philip.
Deception: a novel/Philip Roth.
p.   cm.
I. Title.
PS3568.0855D44   1990
813'.54—dc20   89-49207
CIP
ISBN 0-671-70374-9

An excerpt, adapted from this book, appeared first in *Esquire*.

For David Rieff

"**I'LL** write them down. You begin."

"What's it called?"

"I don't know. What do we call it?"

"The Dreaming-About-Running-Away-To-gether Questionnaire."

"The Lovers-Dreaming-About-Running-Away-Together Questionnaire."

"The Middle-Aged-Lovers-Dreaming-About-Running-Away-Together Questionnaire."

"You're not middle-aged."

"I certainly am."

"You seem young to me."

"Yes? Well, that shall certainly have to come up in the questionnaire. Everything to be answered by both applicants."

"Begin."

"What's the first thing that would get on your nerves about me?"

"When you are at your worst, what is your worst?"

"Are you really this lively? Do our energy levels correspond?"

"Are you a well-balanced and charming extrovert, or are you a neurotic recluse?"

"How long before you'd be attracted to another woman?"

"Or man."

"You must never get older. Do you think the same about me? Do you think about this at all?"

"How many men or women do you have to have at one time?"

"How many children do you want to interfere with your life?"

"How orderly are you?"

"Are you entirely heterosexual?"

"Do you have any specific idea of what interests me about you? Be precise."

"Do you tell lies? Have you lied to me already? Do you think lying is only normal, or are you against it?"

"Would you expect to be told the truth if you demanded it?"

"Would you demand the truth?"

"Do you think it's weak to be generous-minded?"

"Do you care about being weak?"

"Do you care about being strong?"

"How much money can I spend without your resenting it? Would you let me have your Visa card, no questions asked? Would you let me have any power over your money at all?"

"In what ways am I already a disappointment?"

"What embarrasses you? Tell me. Do you even know?"

"What are your real feelings about Jews?"

"Are you going to die? Are you mentally and physically okay? Be specific."

"Would you prefer someone richer?"

"How inept would you be if we were discovered? What would you say if someone came in that door? Who am I and why is it all right?"

"What things don't you tell me? Twenty-five. Any more?"

"I can't think of any."

"I look forward to your answers."

"And I to yours. I have one."

"Yes?"

"Do you like what I wear?"

"That's straining."

"Not at all. The more trivial the defect the more anger it inspires. That's my experience."

"Okay. Last question?"

"I have it. I have it. The last question. Do you in any way, in any corner of your heart, still harbor the illusion that marriage is a love affair? If so, that can be the cause of a lot of trouble."

*

"My husband's girlfriend gave him a present the other day. She's very pretentious, a very jealous and ambitious kind of person. Everything has to be high drama for her. She gave him this record. I can't remember, but it's a very well known, very beautiful piece of music. Schubert—and all about the loss of the greatest passion in his life, the most interesting woman of the century, who was tall and thin—oh, it's all related to that. All this is made very plain in the liner notes, how this is the greatest passion that could ever be conceived, the true marriage of true minds, and all this really high-flown stuff about the misery and ecstasy of being separated by cruel fate. It was so clearly a pretentious gift. He makes the mistake of being open about all these things, you see. He could simply have said that he bought it himself. But he told me that she had given it to him. And I don't think he'd looked at the back. I was drunk one evening, and I've got this pink stuff that you underline with and it makes things stand out. And I underlined about seven phrases that just looked hilariously funny when you did that. Then I calmly withdrew to a dignified distance and handed him the cover of this record. Do you think that was awful of me?"

"Why were you drunk?"

"I wasn't drunk. I'd had a lot of drinks."

"You have a lot to drink at night."

"Yeah."

"How much?"

"Oh, I drink a huge amount. It depends. Some evenings I don't drink anything. But if I were drinking, I could easily drink several doubles be-fore dinner, and several afterwards, and wine in between. I wouldn't even be drunk. I would just be kind of elevated."

"So you don't get much reading done these days."

"No. Though I don't drink by myself. There's someone there when I drink. Though we don't really stay together very much. Well, we have recently—but it's not usual."

"It's such a strange life you lead."

"Yes, it is strange. It's a mistake. But there we are, that's my life."

"How unhappy are you?"

"What I find is that it goes in periods. One has periods of ghastliness. And then long periods of sort of quiet and love. There was a long time when it seemed that all these things were getting worse. And then there was a short time when they seemed to be resolving themselves. And now I think neither of us wishes to have too many confrontations. Because it achieves nothing. And it just makes it all the more difficult to live with each other."

"Do you still sleep together?"

"I thought you were going to ask me that. I'm not going to answer that question. If you want to go somewhere in Europe, I know exactly where I want to go."

"You with me?"

"Ummm. Amsterdam. I've never been there. And there's a wonderful exhibition."

*

"You're looking at the clock to see what time it is."

"People who drink too much often look at the clock before they have their first drink. Just in case."

"What's the matter?"

"Oh, nothing. Two nannies, two children, and two cleaning women all squabbling, and the usual English damp. Then my daughter, since she's been ill, has taken to waking me up at any time, three, four, five. What's tiring is I'm responsible to all my responsibilities. I need a holiday. And I don't think we can continue to have a sexual relationship. The day's too short."

"Is that right? That's too bad."

"No, I don't think we can. Don't you agree, actually? Last time we talked about it, wasn't that the direction in which your own conversation was tending?"

"Oh, I see. This is a preemptive strike. Okay. Whatever you want."

Laughing. "Well, I think that's best. I think that you put yourself very neatly when you said it was driving you nuts."

"What was driving me nuts?"

"Well, all these sexual matters. You said you didn't think you were very keen on just a romantic friendship."

"I see."

"That's sort of your we'll-let-that-ride expression."

"No, no, it's not. It's my I'm-still-listening expression."

"Well, perhaps I shouldn't have simplified like that."

"Really? Oh, I'll simplify it for you, if you want it simple."

"Don't say nothing. I hate you to say nothing."

*

"It's very strange to see you."

"Stranger not to, isn't it?"

"No, I usually *don't* see you."

"You do look a bit different. What's been happening to you?"

"That makes me look so different? You tell me what the difference is and I'll tell you what did it. Am I taller, shorter, fatter, wider?"

"No, it's very subtle."

"Something subtle? Shall I be serious? I missed you."

*

"I went to see a friend of ours who left her husband. She's very clever, she's very beautiful, and she's very successful. And she's extremely courageous and self-disciplined. And she's got lots of money. And she looks terrible."

"How long has she been on her own?"

"Two months."

"She'll look worse."

"Not only does she earn this huge amount of money in an interesting job, but she had a lot of money, so that there are no problems of that sort."

"She have children?"

"She has two children."

"A cautionary visit."

"Well, if she can't do it, well . . . really. She's just been terribly ill, she's moved house, she's just got divorced, and her children are kicking up from being wretched and . . . I couldn't begin. I couldn't begin."

*

"You don't want him to give her up though, do you? You don't want to say, 'If you don't give her up, I'm going to sleep in the other room. You can either fuck me or you can fuck her. Take your choice.' "

"No. No. I think that she's really an important part of his life, and it would not only be mad but selfish."

"Selfish on your part?"

"Yes."

"Really? Is that your point of view? If it is, then you can marry me. That's a lovely point of view—I've never run into it before. A woman saying, 'It would be selfish for me to ask my husband to give up his girlfriend.' "

"I think it would though."

"Usually people think it's selfish of the man to want her and to have her, not selfish of the woman to ask him to give her up."

"A point of view that is reasonable and right doesn't come naturally. That was my first response. But it is what I think . . . I can see that I've behaved very stupidly with my husband, but maybe it's because I don't know what I've done wrong. He has had to put up with years of me being terribly depressed and lonely. I don't think it was entirely surprising—I was alone so much and he was away so much and working so hard. I didn't have other affairs, because I always thought he was vulnerable and had to be protected."

"He doesn't sound that vulnerable to me."

*

"So he's safely in a hospital room. You think the tootsie's over there?"

" 'Tootsie' is such a wonderful word."

"I thought you might like it. You're getting your little vacation finally."

"Well, I think I've given him an unduly bad press. He has many, many qualities. But the truth of the matter is that I haven't slept so well for a long time. I woke up this morning feeling absolutely normal."

*

"Did you listen to the record I gave you?"

"No. I had to hide it."

"Why do you have to hide it?"

"Because it would be unusual for me to buy a record. I don't often do it."

"What are you going to do with it?"

"Well, I'll play it in the evening when I'm alone."

"What are you going to do if it's found? Salt and pepper it and eat it?"

"I did buy records, but I did get so upset for a while that—well, that's history."

"What? Did you have fights about that too?"

"Yes."

"Did you really?"

"Yes."

"That's not necessary."

"No."

*

"You look lovely. That's a nice outfit. Is it on inside out?"

"No. I have lots of clothes with seams on the outside. You never noticed. It's terribly smart. Suggests that you're somewhat anarchic."

"Well, you look lovely but you sound aw-fully tired. And you're getting skinny again. Don't you take vitamins and all the rest of those things?"

"Intermittently I do. It's that I haven't eaten for three days. I'm so busy."

"Too busy."

"Yeah. I'm sitting in this room trying to type, and this little one comes in and first of all she does a pee on the carpet. And then she goes out and she cries some more and then she comes in again. Then she shuffles several pages around, then she takes the telephone off the hook, and then she comes up to me and she does a crap all over my sofa. Then I have to go off to work and make sycophantic noises at my boss for eight hours."

"And the husband?"

"It's easier when I don't see you. One makes an adjustment and places one's distractions elsewhere—and just forgets, you know? You don't get involved in this terrible comparing. I've wanted very much to explain to you what's been going on in my head. But I feel that perhaps I'm abusing you, and I don't want to do that. One thing that I want is to stop having to explain all that shit to you. I will if you ask me but I'd rather not talk about it."

"Talk about it. I like to know what's going on in your head. I'm very fond of your head."

"I just had my mother for the weekend.

And he just disappeared. I had my mother entirely on my own for the weekend. And I haven't slept well for nights. And I think about you a great deal. And tomorrow I have to have lunch with my mother-in-law, which is a slightly grueling experience—she's a woman who can really criticize. She can be so hellishly unpleasant that one tries to keep things out of her way. And the nanny is restive. They all hop around from one house to another, the nannies, comparing employers, and ours becomes very restive. And you know what a cervix is?"

"I think so."

"Such a silly word, 'cervix.' Well, I've got a lump on mine. I have to go have a test or something. And my husband says I've ruined his sex life. He says, 'You're so heavy, everything is so serious, awful, there's no joy, no fun, no humor in anything'—and it's true, I think. I think he exaggerates grossly, but it's truish. I don't enjoy sex at all. It's all rather lonely and hard. But it's like this, life, isn't it?"

"Why don't you do your husband a favor and try to come?"

"I don't want to."

"Do it. Just let yourself do it. It's thought to be better than arguing."

"I get so angry with him."

"Don't get angry. He's your husband. He's fucking you. Let him."

"You mean try harder."

"No. Yes. Just *do* it."

"Those things are not under one's conscious control."

"Yes, they are. Just be a whore for half an hour. It won't kill you."

"Whores don't come. They certainly don't want to."

"*Play* the whore. Don't be so serious about it."

"That's his problem—*he's* so serious about it. He's one of these people who think women should have multiple orgasms and everybody should come together. Well, this is all perfectly normal, and what happens among young people, because it's so easy. But as soon as you've acquired a history and a few resentments—oh, there's *so* much antagonism between us. And why *is* it that one just loses interest utterly in someone sexually?"

"Why don't you ask me why it snows?"

"But it is a reason for leaving him, isn't it?"

"That isn't the reason you're leaving him, if you're even leaving him."

"No. But if I come right down to it, that's what lies underneath it all. He couldn't bear my losing interest in him."

*

"How are you?"

"Oh, busy and angry, as usual."

"You look tired."

"Well, it's not surprising, is it? I've got mascara, I'm afraid, running down my face."

"What are you angry about?"

"I had this terrible scene with my husband. Yesterday. Because it was Valentine's Day and you have to have a scene. Somebody had said to him that he isn't the right husband for me because I really like to be spoiled, and of course I got very indignant—but sometimes I wonder."

"Well, maybe because it was Valentine's Day I woke up in the middle of the night and I had the terrific sensation of your hand on my cock. Now that I think about it, it might have been my hand. But it wasn't—it was yours."

"It was no one's—it was a dream."

"Yes—called 'Be My Valentine.' How did I get so hooked on you?"

"I think it's that you spend all day in this room. Sitting in this room, you don't have any new experience."

"I have you."

"I'm just the same as everything else."

"Oh no you're not. You're lovely."

"Really? Do you think so? I feel a bit ropey, actually. I feel a lot older."

"How long is it now?"

"Us? About a year and a half. I usually
don't do anything for more than two years. I mean
jobs and things. I don't really know anything
about you, you know? Oh, I know a bit about you.
From reading your books. But not a lot. It's difficult to know somebody in one room. We might
as well be holed up in an attic like the Frank
family."

"Well, that's what we're stuck with."

"I suppose. This is life."

"There is no other."

"Why don't you give me a drink?"

"You're near tears, aren't you?"

"Am I? I feel so urgently the need for privacy. I've been longing to sleep alone for as long
as I can remember. No, that's an exaggeration.
But at the end of the day, when I'm really tired
and it's another emotional battle . . . And not only
that, but the distraction of somebody else sleeping
beside me. We have a very big bed, but not big
enough. It's just so sad, isn't it? I mean he has so
many wonderful qualities— May I have that drink,
please? I'm not terribly stable today. I find it absolutely intolerable that he should say to me, 'I've
given up so much for you and it's not worth it.' It's
so painful. And he said that twice in the last couple
of weeks. *Why* can't it get better? We get on so
well! And actually I do care for him. I'd miss him
horribly if I weren't there. There's so much I like

about him. . . . Anyway, I shouldn't go on with you like this."

"Why not?"

"Oh, I don't know what I want."

"What you want is not to be in this situation any longer."

"Is that what I want? Is that it?"

*

"Do you think it would help to see a psychiatrist? Because what I still don't know is what I want. If somebody said to me, 'Look, your husband will stop fooling around, and he will treat you with great respect, and deference, and he'll be utterly charming, but you won't feel different sexually, you're not going to feel any sexual interest, and you're going to have to put up with—"

"Do you feel any interest in anyone?"

"Now, or ever?"

"Both."

"I used to really enjoy it."

"And now? You don't want to make love to me, do you?"

"I don't want to make love to anybody. At all. I don't know the answer to this. I don't think there's anything wrong with me sexually in general. But there certainly is at the moment. I've even got to the stage where it actually hurts."

"The answer to your question about seeing a psychiatrist is yes."

"Somebody good is difficult to find."

"Are you going to do that on the sly, or openly? And if you do it openly, why are you going to say you're doing it?"

"The only reason I wouldn't do it openly is because later it might emerge that I was unfit to be a mother. That I was neurotic and therefore it would be much better if the child were with her father."

"No court would hear it."

"But I don't want to go to court—I just want things to be *different*."

*

"You know what I'm doing on Tuesday? I'm going to see a solicitor."

"About getting divorced?"

"Well, not really about that. Just to find out what's up. I'll probably arrive here in a very heightened state."

"Good. It'll be interesting."

*

"What happens when he asks you how you got that bruise on your thigh?"

"He already did."

"Oh. And?"

"I told the truth. I always tell the truth. That way you never get caught in a lie."

"What did you say?"

"I said, 'I got this bruise in a torrid embrace with an unemployed writer in a walk-up flat in Notting Hill."

"And?"

"It sounds silly and everybody laughs."

"And you maintain the illusion that you're an honest woman."

"Absolutely."

*

"You're trembling. Are you ill?"

"I'm excited."

*

"Do I look horrible?"

"We'll pour some whiskey down you."

"If I start to go through this divorce business, I'm going to have to behave quite impeccably. But I don't think I'm going to do it."

"Then don't do it."

"I don't know what my intentions are. It was rather a strain telling all these things to some lawyer. What I found offensive is that he had some very attractive young girl lawyer there as well. I nearly said she must go and then I thought we better not start off like that. I decided that I wasn't going to go into any confessions or anything. But there are certain things you cannot avoid, like 'Has your husband committed adultery?' "

"What did you say?"

"I said yes. He has for years. Well, if you put up with someone's adultery for six months, you condone it. And it can no longer be a cause in itself. They were quite curious to know why I put up with it. So I said, forget that, it's really this: he has this wonderful setup where he can do exactly what he likes, and I have discovered that this is a terribly unusual setup, and if I can't get something like that going on my side, I think I might as well call it a day. And this girl was shocked that I was being so frivolous. But it's very difficult to discuss these things. You don't really want to talk to them about it."

"But you have to."

"You know, once upon a time when I lived in the country, and before I spent a lot of time in the city, I felt simple and I wished to be simple. But that dies if you struggle a lot. I used to be a lot of fun."

"I enjoy you now."

"I'm kind of grieving today over the fact

that we don't have any kind of sexual life. I mean, whatever sexual life we have is not what *I* want."

"You tell the lawyers?"

"That? No, of course not. He's very keen on sex, but from my point of view, the way it's all worked out, there's nothing in it."

"You told me. You endure it."

"Well, not even that anymore. I've decided to give it up."

"So that's going to bring the end about even if the lawyers don't."

"I know. But it just seemed too stupid. Funnily enough, oddly enough, I think there's something to be said for . . ."

"Celibacy?"

"I wasn't going to say that, though I think that's also true. It's much better for working—I have a lot more ideas. And feel much more in control of myself. And have much more access to all the things I want to think about. And am not so terribly distracted as I was. What happens, I think, is that you sort of close down shop, sexually. You go into hibernation. I don't know because I haven't done it before. It's not really natural to me. I used to be sexually quite arrogant because it was all so easy."

"Once upon a time."

"Yeah."

"I AM Czechoslovakian girl, graduate of Russian literature. I emigrated to U.S.A. in 1968 after the Russian tanks come. I lived in U.S.A. for six years, in Upper East Side, and now I come back."

"Welcome."

"I fell hopelessly in love with my new home in '68. Everything in America was new—I had to learn many things and I had to be fast. I studied acting but I did not go any further than to bikini test for Paramount. So I went into fashion but I was not so happy with that job, so I would like to write book now. This is why I come to see you."

"I'm glad you did, though I don't know if I can help."

"When I arrived in U.S.A. I worked at first for television producer and lived in his town house as live-in baby-sitter. I thought this is America. When I left this house I found myself apartment in East Side. I found that my body was out of the usual. They invited me for modeling. They put me in silk robe embroiled with gold. I look down at what he is doing and I saw his big big penis and he was waiting if I look for the penis or if I keep myself busy with modeling robe. I did not go for the penis, so he ask for my girlfriend. It was clear to me that I will have to make life at my own."

"How did you do that?"

"The man who I was meeting got me new apartment in celebrity building. Across from live beautiful black model. I saw the beautiful black man taking out her garbage. I will always run just to stay next to them in the elevator. Actor who live in that building also take me visit to his girlfriend. He will make love to the two of us and then make climaxed only the other girl. I was despaired. The man was doing that to me everywhere. Some of my girlfriend become prostitutes. They will come

home in the morning with pocketbook full of
hundred-dollar bills. I succeed to get job as a bra
model. They put at me black Valentino dress on I
did model. I kept the dress and start to visit bars
in the Hotel Pierre and Plaza. What are men like?
Will they like me?"

"Did they?"

"Men like me too much. I started to hate
my body. I will tight my big breast under the
clothes, I will go to take voice and speech lessons
just to loose my accent. As I found out the accent
was doing that to me too. But there was still my
off-white complexion left. I started to hate money.
Anything I dream about was love. I think I will go
to the Sigmund Freud doctor."

"You got therapy."

"No. I become party girl. The man took me
to show business party, call girls party, United Na-
tion party. I become jet-setter. I will fly to Aca-
pulco and beautifully wasted my time. I run in
fifty-four-year-old Belgian millionaire and for two
years we entertain our self as what the money can
buy and where ever in beautiful place its can take
you. You know the mentality; he will go in bed with
half of the disco but always leave with me. I
started to do the same, as I felt I was woman and
it was time of women's liberation. Fulfillment to
me was trip to Monte Carlo, Regine's disco, five
beautiful lovers calling my apartment in Fifth Av-

enue, Parke-Bernet, couturier clothes, French restaurants, et cetera. My life was quite meaningless but it was always better than to marry poor man, live in Brooklyn, and have three children. All over I felt it was all the time the same. Only the decorations changed. With the bill being served to my boyfriend. We both started to dream about foreign places and foreign people. As everybody who watched me started to talk about his airplane and take out his money or credit cards. I became very curious about the sex and I start to experimentize at my own, as I saw everybody to do that. I got myself the best the Manhattan can offer to me. I end up in hospital with the emotional illness."

"For how long?"

"Two months. I come out. Living the flashy life, I always keep study. I become professional apartment decorator, I went to school to become fashion designer, I took French cooking courses, finishing school for young ladies. I work with discipline. And as the miracles are often achieved with the discipline it happen with me."

"And the discipline—that's the happy end of the story?"

"No. No, no. In Regine's disco in Monte Carlo I met beautiful stranger and I let myself to fall hopelessly in love with him. He was Arab. I live with him one year in style in Paris, where I go to French classes and he marry me. I went to live

with him Kuwait. There was a price for a thousand
and one nights. I kept fainting all over the place.
Bang, and I was just right at the floor. He turned
into the hard, intelligent, brutal man. Then the
Palestinian raped me, they told me that my husband was paid to marry me. They took me into the
Embassy, they told me that my husband was Com-
munist and they offer me to sign contract for two
hundred thousand dollars. I found the connection
between the ambassador to the United Nations
who I kept meeting at the Upper East Side parties.
They follow me. Communists. I run up to the
Czechoslovakian Embassy. They already know
everything. I was set up. They said, 'You go to
U.S.A. and work for us. You go and beat the
Jews.' "

"That doesn't entirely surprise me."

"They took me to police station and beat
criminal in front of me until I fainted. I ran to the
United Nations, the committee for human rights.
They said, we cannot do anything for you. It is
criminal intent to the United States security."

"I don't follow you."

"They said, you are very important political
witness. I remember all this years being outsider
in the society and now there was not even law for
me."

"And what are you asking of me?"

"Please, I love Kafka and I studied Freud.

And I love and deeply respect Jewish people. I admire their intelligence. I am looking for somebody who will read and help me with my book."

"Your book is about what?"

"There was not in the history published book about prostitute written by prostitute. I need to found somebody who will help me to get published. I will be so glad if it could be you."

"**YOU** think Jews in England try harder?"

"I do."

"But it's not hard to try harder in England."

"Nonsense. Really, your picture of the English is very different from mine."

"The lowest production rate per capita in the world is in England."

"You're talking about industrial workers. And they're very smart. Why should they work? But people who actually have something to gain by working in this country, they work. And I've seen them do it."

"And the Jews work even harder than these people."

"No. I just said they tried harder than I did."

"Do you have a Jewish woman friend?"

"No. Obviously not a close one, or I could think of her. I'm trying to think of a less close one. I've had [*laughing*] close Jewish men friends."

*

"Which do you prefer?"

"I don't wish to talk about this."

"But I want to know. Which do you prefer?"

"For fondling, the uncircumcised. It's interesting to move the sheath over the head."

"And for fucking?"

"You can't ask this of a nicely brought-up English female."

"For fucking."

"The circumcised."

"Why?"

"It's like having it naked."

"The naked penis."

"I guess."

*

"Honestly, I swear to you that it's true. I never masturbated until I was twenty-seven."

"Poor you."

*

"Close your eyes."

"Uh-oh."

"Close 'em."

"I am not going to be tied up."

"My dear friend, who here ever suggested tying you up this early in the game?"

"I've read about it in books."

"So?"

"Writers write those books."

"Close your eyes."

"If I must."

"Let's see how much attention you've been paying. Describe this room."

"To begin with, it's far too small for two people to conduct a love affair in."

"Can't we find a house with a bed in it?"

"No. We can't. I've thought about it. I have friends with houses with beds in them but I don't

see how we could. There are cleaning ladies, nannies, children—"

"Then this little room without a bed will
have to do, won't it?"

"It does have two nice French windows
looking out on a green lawn and a flowering tree.
In keeping with the room's functional austerity,
the windows have neither shades nor curtains, so
that the people in the houses across the garden, I
am quite certain, can clearly see everything that is
going on."

"Mostly what they see is someone typing.
Sometimes they see him reading. Anything more
interesting they deserve."

"There is a very comfortable black leather
chair in which a woman who should be back at
work is sitting. Wearing two rubber bands around
his wrist, bending and twisting the paper clips with
which he constantly fidgets while he listens to the
woman complain about her marriage, is a man in a
leather desk chair. His desk, about three by five,
consists of a gray metallic pedestal and a pale For-
mica top whose surface is not as orderly as his
compulsiveness would lead you to expect, though
he seems to know which uneven pile of papers is
unfinished manuscript and which is a stack of un-
answered letters and which contain the clippings
about Israel that he cuts from the London papers
to prove to her that the British are anti-Semitic.

The typewriter, on a typing desk placed at right angles to the writing desk, is an IBM Correcting Selectric Two. Black and serious. A Prestige Pica Seventy-two golf ball."

"Very good."

"Bookshelves built into the wall behind the desk. Much complaining about shoddy British workmanship while construction was under way. Books: *Heine's Jewish Comedy* by Prawer, *The Jew as Pariah* by Hannah Arendt, *White Nights* by Menachem Begin—on and on. Entirely too many books about Jews, by Jews, for Jews. A dusty, torn Japanese paper globe suspended over the desk, property of previous tenant. Two chrome architect lamps, or whatever they're called, one for each desk. Two Dimplex heating units, white. Commercial carpet, steel blue. One plastic mat for back exercises and adultery. Various London literary weeklies stacked beside Roberts radio tuned to Radio Three on cheap glass-and-bamboo coffee table. Paris edition of *Herald Tribune* open and folded back to sports page. One extra-large wicker wastebasket stuffed with *Herald Tribune* back issues, discarded work sheets, torn manuscript pages; also several Spud-U-Like cardboard containers for baked potatoes with ratatouille filling, signifying lunch is as Spartan as everything else. Plaster floral ornamentation on ceiling molding the sole voluptuous detail."

"That all?"

"Unfortunately. Now you close your eyes."

"Okay."

"Let's see how much attention *you've* been paying."

"Go ahead."

"Describe me."

*

"I made such a fuss about what they're going to do with the baby if there's anything wrong with it. I wanted a doctor who would bump it off. I found several. I just went to these doctors and said, what would you do if there was something seriously wrong with the baby. Obviously they're not going to bump off a child who looks healthy just because you're afraid it might be brain damaged. But a spina bifida child or a mongol or certain very gross obvious problems. And I know what I'm talking about. I talked to four doctors. What was interesting at the time and why I was particularly upset about it was because there were two cases, just before I was due. One was where a guy did murder a child and he was convicted of it. Of murder. There was tremendous controversy. All over the papers. He was recognized to be a fanatically devoted, decent man. He'd brought up a handicapped child himself, so though he had killed

it he was left off. But he had done it. He hadn't
intervened and he hadn't given the child enough
nourishment. But it takes ages if you're going to
starve them. You have to really beat their heads in
if you're going to be serious about it. You can murder them or you can let them die. And the awful
thing is that babies who have something seriously
wrong with them are often very strong—otherwise
they'd have died in the womb or been aborted. The
other case was when a woman with a mongol child
had to give it up and somebody adopted it after
she'd tried to murder it. There are lots of creeps
who want to raise handicapped children."

"You're not one."

"Are you? You don't even want to raise a
healthy child. The first doctor I went to, a very
decent man, he said he agreed to my attitude but
he wouldn't risk his career for it. And that's that.
One of them said that of course he agreed with me
and I shouldn't worry. Babies could easily be dis-
posed of by shoving surgical swabs down their
throats until they choked. So I said I thought that
was rather excessive, there must be kinder ways
of murdering babies. The nicest man and the best
doctor said yes, and he clearly would have done
something terribly painful for himself and difficult
—oh, I did worry about it a lot. And there was
something else I'd found out, which was sustain-
ing. Which is that if you're a woman and you com-

mit any crime within six weeks of giving birth, you almost certainly will not even go to court about it. Because there's a dispensation in law that women in that period, and even within a year of giving birth—well, they consider that you're slightly off your head. So you could murder it and you'd get away with it, I think. You'd have to be damn careful, but I do think you would get away with it."

*

"You're not saying much. You hardly do, you know, when I'm here."

"I'm listening. I listen. I'm an écouteur— an audiophiliac. I'm a talk fetishist."

"Ummm. It *is* erotic, you just sitting there listening."

"Not so odd, really."

"It isn't, is it?"

*

"We used to have the television in the bedroom and everybody used to come and watch it in this huge double bed we have. It was the beginning of so many destructive alliances. For the sake of the community we took it out of the bedroom. At least three couples found each other watching telly on our double bed."

"Sounds like a nice idea."
"No, it wasn't very helpful."

*

"Last Sunday you said, 'I have to go home because he'll get curious.' Why do you care if he gets curious?"

"Because I have to tell lies and I don't like doing it. I have to preserve some sense of truth without actually getting caught, and it's extremely irritating. Tedious. It is. I have plenty of other plans to make without having to construct a hundred little red herrings."

*

"It's very cozy with you on a snowy day. Lying just like this and all the snow going round the trees—quite wonderful."

*

Undressing him. "This is a new belt."

*

After he comes. Softly. "Are you all right?"
"Sweet girl."

"What are you thinking?"

"No thoughts. Isn't that nice?"

"It's sublime."

*

"Do you honestly have thoughts about jumping out a window?"

"Oh yes."

"A lot?"

"Frequently."

"And what stops you?"

"It isn't that I want to die, it's that I want to live—to live better. I want life to be better, so I realize I better stay in it for a while longer."

*

"There was a crime prevention officer at home. *And* my husband. So they held me up a bit."

"Are you okay?"

"Yes, I am. May I sit down, please?"

"Yes, you sit down right there, miss."

"I was very surprised to find these two men at home."

"I like 'crime prevention officer.' "

"I know. How about that. But he didn't have my crime in mind. There's been a rape in our road. Next door, in fact. So I was worried about our house, which is full of windows. And we have this very attractive young girl, our nanny. So the police came around to see me. A very handsome young police officer, out of uniform, came to see me. He wanted to have a chat."

"What's a crime prevention officer?"

"He wants to prevent crime. He wants to prevent, in particular, the crime of anybody breaking into our house. Because it's not properly fortified."

"But Banham's does this."

"But I had them to do it. They did such a bad job that I can get in myself."

"And rape yourself."

"I've got other things to do when I'm at home. So that's why I'm late. It took me aback."

"So how did you get out?"

"Well, it was really quite difficult, because my husband was expecting that I'd come home from work and stay and have tea with the baby."

"So what did you say?"

"I said I was going out."

"And he said?"

"Where to? And I said, I'm not going to tell you. But in a very friendly way. And—so I went. And here I am."

"Irritated with me because you had to go through all that to get here."

"I'm not."

"Okay."

"I don't think I'm irritated."

"Well, let's find out."

*

"Did you get my letter?"

"Yes, I did. It was wonderful. I tore it up. I thought that would be the perfect thing to do."

*

"It's five o'clock. Time you Gentiles start drinking, isn't it?"

"I think so."

"Very impressive."

"What?"

"You with your hair up."

"It doesn't suit me."

"It suits *me*."

"Why aren't you happy with your wife? Why isn't it enough?"

"Why isn't your husband enough?"

"I told you a great deal about him. I want to hear about you. I've told you plenty about myself. I want to know why she isn't enough."

"You're asking the wrong question."

"What's the right question?"

"I don't know."

"Why am I here?"

"Because I followed temptation where it led me. I do that now that I'm older."

"All of this sounds like a popular song."

"That's why they're popular."

"Why are you so anxious to avoid wounding her?"

"Why should I want to wound her?"

"I didn't mean that you would or you should. But since you don't seem free to do anything . . ."

"What's free? You?"

"Freeish. Free-er."

"Nonsense."

"But if you care about somebody enough to want to protect her . . . I just wonder why she should be in such a vulnerable position."

"You're being euphemistic."

"I'm not."

"Then I don't understand."

"I would have thought that she would keep your attention, more of your attention, than she seems to have. And it seems odd that she hasn't. But then people say the same of me, I suppose. I mean, about my husband."

"Perhaps we should give this conversation up."

"Why, when there are things about you I want to know?"

"Perhaps it works better if only one participant in an adulterous affair complains about domestic dissatisfactions. If both go at it, it's unlikely there'd be time for the thing itself."

"So your dissatisfactions are out of bounds. Except your dissatisfactions with England and Englishness."

"Isn't it possible that domestic dissatisfaction—as distinct from cultural displacement—has nothing to do with having fallen in love with you? Isn't it possible that I'm not as burdened by all that as you are and consequently have less to say about it? Isn't it possible that my predicament lies elsewhere?"

"It's cultural displacement that's driven you into this—is that what you're telling me?"

"Maybe something like that."

"Could you be a little more specific, please?"

"As they say in an idiom more succinct than our own, *Il faut coucher avec sa dictionnaire.*"

"So our story isn't a love story, really—it's a cultural story. That's the one that interests you."

"That one always interests me."

"That explains the Gentile women, does it? You fall in love for the anthropology."

"Could be worse. There are other ways of addressing anthropological differences, you know.

There's the old standby hatred. There's xenopho-
bia, violence, murder, there's genocide—"

"So, you're kind of the Albert Schweitzer
of cross-cultural fucking."

Laughing. "Well, not *so* saintly. The Mali-
nowski will do."

"**I WAS** a little Czech girl and I came to your hotel and you wanted me to go up to your room to get some books to help you to carry. It was ten o'clock in the morning. They were very rude. They treated me like a whore and then you made a scene. Then I took you across the Charles Bridge. And you taught me all those colloquial words. We had dinner in your hotel. You didn't particularly care about me, because when I came to your hotel you were sitting and drinking something. I was about twenty-one, twenty-two. I'm much older now."

"What's the name of that park, at the top of Prague, where we sat?"

"I don't know. We didn't go there. It must have been someone else."

"No, no one else. I particularly *did* care for you."

"You telephoned me once to invite me to an orgy. Remember? And I said I could only watch. And you said, no, you have to participate. So I wasn't brave enough to go."

"You didn't miss anything."

"You were followed all the time and when we sat in a restaurant this chap sat with us and we just couldn't take it. Working in the American Library wasn't a very clever thing for me to do. My professor got me the job. He said, almost as a joke, it would be nice for all of us, because we could get books and we can't go there. We all thought I'd be sitting in a library and working with books and reading. Which for two years it was. It was a great job, fantastic job, but in the end it started to be difficult. I had to decide whether I work for Secret Service or go. I'm not supposed to talk about it still."

"You're in London. It's okay. Talk."

"How I got the job, I went to see the cultural attaché. And he said, 'Oh, I'd be interested in you because you studied literature and so on.' He was a very nice man. Of Czech origin. So I liked him and he liked me, and he gave me a job, no trouble. But then you have to go to the Czech organization, who either give it to you or not. It organizes all employees for any foreign work, which in reality is a branch of Secret Service. Which I didn't know. I was just a stupid little girl and I was very excited about the job. I thought it would be great, I'll be in contact, it's exactly what I studied. And I had some nice friends, and I was popular, but the more I was popular with Americans, the more I was in trouble. This organization, they let me work for two years and then they call me back and they said, 'Oh, we're sure you like your job, also you have much more money in that job than anywhere else and lots of other perks.' And then they count on your not being brave enough to leave but staying and working for them. And also it's very difficult to leave because after that nobody will employ me as a teacher. First they give me a piece of paper to sign, saying that this discussion we were about to have was a state secret and that if I ever tell anybody about it, I can be put in prison. I could be put in prison anyway because I talk to my girlfriends, to several people, because I was so scared. I was informed that this discussion is under paragraph such and such and it's a state secret. And if I reveal it to anybody, including my own family, I can be prosecuted and in prison up to seven years. I said, 'What do you want me to do?' and they said they won't tell me until I sign. So I said, 'I can't sign anything I don't know about.' So they said, 'Do you want a few days to decide?' And I said, 'No, I can tell you straight-away. I can't do it, I don't want to do it.' So they said, 'You'll have to find yourself another job. Be-cause it's no future for you in the library.' They didn't fire me, they said I'd have to find another job. They didn't do anything to me, they just said there was no future for me and that I eventually had to leave. I went back to work and I didn't tell anybody. On top of it, the Americans then did the same thing. Told me that they were very interested in me. And the same thing, I refused as well. They didn't want me to sign something, they just asked me to work for them. I said no, I didn't want to do it. So by that time, my situation started to be ab-solutely awful. On both sides. They both were in-terested in me because I speak the languages. I speak German as well. So probably I would be suitable for them. I was quite good at translating. I always enjoyed literature and translated stories for Czech newspapers. So since then I started being not very welcome from both of them. I left very soon afterwards. I left and I was forgotten. Fortunately I found a teaching job. For another two years I did that—then I married. He came to Czechoslovakia and he married me. In between I was in love with an American professor who was very serious but I was not permitted to see him— the Czechs wouldn't let me go out and he lived in Toronto. And also he was getting divorced and didn't know what to do and I was very upset about men who don't know what they want to do. So I married this stupid Englishman who at least knew he wanted me. 1978. It was absolutely silly because he was an easygoing English- man who all he likes is the football and cricket. He's this type who will go to pubs—I had quite an interesting half year seeing horses and dogs and pubs. I can't blame him, I can only blame myself."

"You married him to get out."

"I don't know, because I was longing for something nice, something . . . And I didn't even like him by the time I was leaving Czechoslovakia because I hadn't seen him all year. It took me over a year to get out. To sort all my papers, because, you know, you must have hundreds of papers, you have to pay for your education. When I came to England he was so upset when I was crying, and I was miserable, and I couldn't cope. I just couldn't cope, it was so difficult. And he started to hate me. I was supposed to be very happy that he rescued me from a dreadful, awful country. And I wasn't.

I was miserable and awful and missing all my friends. You probably never met certain English people, because you always move in circles that are different—they're interesting, educated people. But if you get among ordinary people, who may be quite nice, but you just talk a different language . . . You just have nothing in common. It was so awful for me to try to live here and to try to get various jobs, and then you mention that you just arrived in England, and nobody wants you. So that was very difficult. I did all possible jobs, typing and selling books at Foyle's—I was thrown out on the third day because the manager was unbearable and I talked back, which you don't do in this country. So I was sacked. But I was still myself. I was still like a Czech. Please, I don't feel like telling you my life story. I told you already in Prague."

"Then it was a different story."

"You should tell me your life story. It's more interesting."

"It's not. Go on."

"He was not a bad man—but I was somebody straight from Czechoslovakia, straight from —well, I always had a rather nice life there, an easy life, apart from those few times I was bothered by the Secret Service. But they didn't do me any harm. They just asked me if I would work for them, I said no, and I think they more or less let me alone. But I was frightened just that they were there. I actually first met them when I met you. When I was caught with you in the hotel, they called me straight when you left for the airport. And wanted to ask me lots of questions about you. I was absolutely terrified then. I was very scared. My hands were trembling. They asked me what I was doing in the hotel with you. And how did I come to get to know you. And if I slept with you. Imagine, I was only twenty-one. They just took me to their offices. To this building. Suddenly they were on my doorstep, showed me the badge, and took me away. I said to them, 'I met him, I spoke to him, I liked him, that's all.' They questioned me not very long, about an hour. One was sort of threatening and one was nice. You know, they have these roles. This was my first time. You always hear about these people in Czechoslovakia, but you never meet them. But this was *me*, and I was sitting there, not knowing what was going to happen to me. I was too young to realize that they can't really do much to me. Now I'm not scared when I see them but at the time I was. You know, I felt dreadful because all I did was go to your room and you said could I help you with some books. That's how they know who I was—because they took my identity card, took my name and address and everything, and apparently just when you left . . . and I was very fond of you, I don't know, there was something nice about you, I liked you very much, in fact. At first I didn't but then you walked across the Charles Bridge, I was sort of—it was just a very nice thing for me to go with somebody whose book I read. One of them said, 'You better tell us everything because we know everything anyway.' To which I answered, 'If you know everything, why do you ask it? Why do you ask me when you know?' They didn't ask me anything about you. They mainly were interested in whether I slept with you. Maybe they thought that somebody who writes a book like this must be a sex maniac. They take any small bit about anybody. So you caused it all—you have to buy me a drink."

"How did it end with the English husband?"

"I saw this advertisement, that they want guides who speak languages. And I went for an interview and it was a Greek, this guy, with dark eyes, a nice man. English people, I hated them at that time, because they are so polite, but just when I would open my mouth and they would hear my foreign accent, I had no chance. And I couldn't prove that I was rather intelligent, because they couldn't care less. Because he was a Greek he said he didn't like the English either and he gave me the job straightaway. So I was delighted, I was absolutely thrilled that finally after one year I got

something to do and make a bit of money. I told
him I was married and I wanted to do just a few
tours because I couldn't do it all the time. And he
agreed, this manager, it was okay, I could do just
a few tours. So I came home and I said to William
that I took it, and he said, 'Well, you decided you
want the job?' And I said, 'I do,' and he said,
'Well, pack up your things and get out of my flat.'
So I did and that was that. It wasn't much fun
because it was about eleven o'clock at night. And
I was sitting on my cases out in the street. On the
one hand I was very happy because I was out of
something I didn't want to be. But it wasn't much
fun, because a Czech girl sitting on her cases
eleven o'clock at night in London . . . Well, I telephoned a girlfriend who was Czech and who also
had a difficult experience here, but she emigrated
in 1968, when the Russians invaded our country,
she didn't speak the language, so she understood.
She said, 'Oh, I expected this telephone call for a
long time. Stay there,' and she and her boyfriend
came and picked me up. And put me up for a few
days. So I was very lucky. Then I just arranged to
see the manager and told him I had nowhere to go,
so I arranged to work all through the season. And
I did so, sleeping in various hotels, every night in
a different bed. I got stubborn. I could have
packed it up and go home. And start all over again.
But there was something in me—I went through

this, I bought a flat, and then I fell in love with someone whom I loved very much but he was married. So that was the saddest thing for me. It only finished recently. It just didn't work. In the beginning it was very beautiful. He very much wanted both. He had two children. He was forty-five. He was very clever and interesting and nice. He was one of the managers of my company. Quite important job. For about a year he was totally in love with me. But it went all wrong because he started to be scared. You know, in England they so very much are in love with their little house—and the *garden*. And wife. And he has kids. I didn't want to marry. I just wanted to be with him. I just wanted him to love me. I could feel how I was losing, because his wife started to say, 'I'm going to destroy you.' At the beginning he said to me that they were sort of separated. Then it was awful, it really was. I nearly went the wrong way. But I actually made it work. Though she started to be so worried that she would lose her husband and all her money. But money was not what I cared for. I wanted him. But what was tragic was that I started slowly to see how I was losing. Because I didn't want to fight. I wanted him to love me because he loved me, not because I would trick him into it. She was clever, she used every technique against me. She knew about me. I even saw her a couple of times. She just came to see me. To talk to me.

To say that she was going to destroy us. But I was
very strong, because I didn't care. I didn't have
anything anyhow. I'm thirty-two, and when you get
to this age you discover . . ."

"Discover what? What have you discovered?"

"I always was trying to be more or less like
other people and worried what they think about
me. Now I know I'm different. I want to be myself.
I want somebody who's going to love me, whom
I'm going to love. I'm not necessarily going to be
married to someone, I just want . . . But people
here, or people anywhere, have rules. I hate
Czechoslovakia because it has very set rules. You
can't breathe. I don't particularly like England because it has another set of rules. Of little houses
and little vegetable gardens, and all their life is to
get something like that. I can't be like that. You
know, that man made me welcome. Because he is
very much interested in the war and East Europe.
And he knew a lot about it. He wasn't like the
majority of people here, who are typically English
and don't know much about the outside world. He
knew what I was like and we could talk about a lot
of things. It was wonderful. I felt totally different,
I enjoyed being here. That's why I was so hurt,
because I'm back being a—well, now again, I have
my distance. I hate my distance. Because I was
educated I more belong to the class that I don't

have the money to be in. I have much more in common with these people than with the people I belong to because of money. I'm misplaced. Totally."

"YOU got thinner."

"No, you've just grown used again to some-body heavier."

"Well, I've got much fatter."

"Have you? It's nice to see you."

"I wish you could have come skiing. I hurt my knee so badly on Thursday that I spent two days lying on the sofa. But it's still a wonderful thing to do. It's so peaceful. Going up the hill very quietly on the lift. And a lot of snow so you couldn't see very well. Just the hiss of your skis."

"Did you have any new thoughts?"

"Thoughts? No. You can't think on the slopes. It's too frightening and too exciting. I had the most thoughtless time. Our friends had an existentialist nephew of twenty-two visiting. Telling us all about why we didn't exist. Or did. It was a little too much. We said, 'Look, we're sorry, but we've read all this too. Leave us alone. We don't want to sit here suffering all the time—we want to go skiing.' You've been with me on a lot of mountains."

"Me?"

"Yes. While riding the T-bar."

"Me and the hiss."

"That's right."

*

"I want some lunch, actually."

"I can give you bits and pieces of things."

"Can you?"

"We'll see if we can put something together for you. Everything all right at home?"

"Yes, it is. It's fine."

"Nothing better for a marriage than an old boyfriend on the side."

"Is that what you think?"

"You want to play reality shift?"

"Maybe."

*

"My mother taught me never to sit with my cunt exposed."

"And your legs over a gentleman's shoulders."

"She never told me that. I don't think she had any idea I'd go in for that."

*

"It's called Jack Daniel's. Smell it."

"Ummm. It does smell good."

*

"I'll tell you an experience that was shocking. To smell this woman's scent on my baby. And the final irony is that it used to be a scent I wore when I was much younger."

"He likes it."

"He doesn't even know that's why he likes it so much. I got tired of it and stopped wearing it, and then it became very popular. It's screamingly popular. It's called Fiji. These things have a scarcity value. If you can smell it in every shop, then it doesn't have et cetera et cetera. But *he* gave it to me."

*

"I feel as though I don't have a cunt. I left my cunt behind today. I don't want to be reminded about it."

"Okay."

"You want me to go?"

"Hardly. You're near tears again today."

"I do feel a bit teary, yes. Can I have something to eat?"

"Well, there are some strawberries, and some melons, and there's some bread, and there's wine, and there's marijuana."

"Can I have a little of each, please?"

*

"You don't also have to fuck when your mother's there, do you? Can't you at least get out of that?"

"No. I have to do everything. Fucking, sucking. Everything. Cooking. There are all these substances in and out of people's mouths. It does sometimes feel that way. I have to make everything right and happy. A barrel of fun."

"It's hard to provide fun."

"It certainly is."

"Maybe you should just become a hooker."

"Oh, I don't think I'd be a very good hooker."

"You'd be a marvelous hooker."

"Yes? What kind of business would I have? I don't think I fit into the general whatever it is, you know, that people have about hookers."

"Are you kidding?"

"I'd have to be a kind of matron type, wouldn't I?"

"Oh, I see—in the sense of people who want discipline. The la-di-da accent and the cool gaze."

"Yes. Who want to have a respectable schoolmistress show them how."

"Yes, you might be able to make money that way."

"Ummm. I would like the money. It's a thought."

*

"Suppose I were to die and a biographer were to go through my notes and come upon your name. He asks, 'Did you know him?' Would you talk?"

"Depends how intelligent he was. If it were someone really serious, yes, I might talk to him. I might say, 'You're going to have to let me see everything in his notebooks before I decide whether to talk to you.' "

" 'He liked you quite a bit, I can tell you that. Can you tell me something about him?' "

"Why are you doing this?"

"I'm curious. 'I want to get this right and you can help me. I have a lot to lose if I get it wrong, and so does he. And so do you. He was big on candor, so why not help me get it right?' "

"If I thought the man was just an idiot, I wouldn't talk to him, because he'd get it even further wrong. What would be the point?"

"Take the best case, not the worst."

"Yeah, well, I might talk to him."

"What would you tell him?"

" 'He didn't write any of his books. They were written by a series of mistresses. I wrote the last two and a half. And even those notes he took down in his hand are my dictation.' "

" 'Look, miss, you're very sweet and pretty, and maybe we can have lunch sometime and you can charm me like this again. But you're not telling me the truth. What kind of affair did you have with him?' "

" 'Very occasional.' "

" 'Was he in love with you?' "

" 'I don't know the answer to that.' What he'd really want to know is what you were really like. What I thought you were really like. I'd be quite good on that."

"Would you?"

"Yes."

"What's the answer?"

"Well, there's no short answer."

" 'You were going to tell me what he was like.' "

" 'I'm not going to tell you. Even if I did, you'd get it wrong in the book.' "

" 'What was he like to you?' "

" 'He was very nice.' "

" 'Nice? That isn't what I've heard. What was he like?' "

" 'A tall, thin man with a cheap watch.' "

" 'Did you want to marry him?' "

"This is a very handy device to get me to reveal myself, isn't it? But I ain't talking. It has to be Leon Edel or I'm not saying a thing."

*

"I find it bloody embarrassing to think that you might be clutching yourself with one hand and the telephone with the other. You don't do that."

"Not with you, toots."

"I'm glad to hear it. I don't think that's quite on."

"It's been done."

"Oh, I know. I know it's commonly done. Giving good phone."

"You told me I give good phone."

"Yes. But I don't necessarily give as good as I get."

*

"You remember me."

"Yes, it's coming back slowly."

"Okay. Take your time."

*

"What can I do for you today?"

"I would like a drink."

"It's got beautiful out."

"Is it? I wasn't noticing."

"You don't look too cheerful."

"We went to dinner on Saturday night. And —I love dancing."

"I didn't know that."

"Disco dancing. I'm really very good at it. I think I'm unusually good at it. I don't very often like to do it because I think it's a form of sexual display. And it's very confusing when you're making sexual displays all over the place. I think it's terribly sexy—and I don't know quite what to do about that. So I have to be quite drunk to do it.

And also, this is true, I've never quite enjoyed disco dancing with my husband. Although he's extremely fit and well built and graceful, it's never struck me the right way. And he's always known this even though I've tried to disguise it. And also there's only one nightclub that we belong to and I think it's very dull and middle-aged. I mean very very middle-aged. It's people taking whores there. I say this because it's necessary to understand the story. But the fact of the story is that we went to a dinner party with old friends, all rather laid back and left wing. Hangovers from the late sixties. People who never really grew up—most of them never married or had children. There was a very attractive young girl sitting next to my husband. She looked a little bit like my husband's girlfriend. The long and short of it is that he took her off to a nightclub. Pissed off in the middle of dinner, not just after pudding, and he sort of excluded me from the invitation in an extremely subtle way. He pissed off well before the end of the evening with one of the guests! Against the will of everybody there."

"Were you embarrassed?"

"No, I wasn't embarrassed—I can't afford to be embarrassed. I wanted to be very embarrassed, if you know what I mean."

"I know what you mean. Was there a man there for you?"

"Well, some were unattached. It was sort of a mixed bag. So I got very upset. Though you must at one level, I think, admire the style and the will. And he looked so utterly charming doing it. Couldn't wait to go dancing, he was so bored with all this stuff."

"Did he fuck her?"

"Don't think so, but I didn't ask."

"And may I ask what you think about all this?"

"I got terribly upset, the most awful feelings. We had the most awful scene when he came home."

"What time?"

"About three-thirty."

"He fucked her. And what then—did he fuck you too?"

"No, certainly not. This is his answer: 'You don't like dancing with me. You don't fancy me. Don't be hypocritical about it. Don't demand from me things that you don't give yourself.' We had a long conversation, of course, very serious."

"How angry were you?"

"I was absolutely furious. But why *should* he be tied to somebody, you know . . ."

"Why should you for that matter?"

"I'm terribly angry with him. But it's true that I'm not in a position to get angry—that's the awful part. It's very difficult, I must say. How does one deal with these things? I have absolutely

no feeling for him at all—at all. Yet this terrible
jealousy I feel—what is it? What's the message,
doctor?"

"My sweet girl, the message is that you
have a choice, you have an option, but one that's
unacceptable to you."

"What's that?"

"Guess."

"He always does these things when I'm so
defenseless. When I'm on top of the world he
behaves beautifully. But as soon as it looks as
though I'm going to be without a job, or I have a new
baby—"

"Or you don't have a lover."

"Or whatever—but what can I do? I could
take the view that I'm onto a very good thing, that
he can do whatever he likes as long as he behaves
nicely—"

"And pays the bills."

"And pays the bills."

"Perhaps you could reach that arrange-
ment. You're very good at articulating the terms of
things aloud."

"Can I ask you something? Why shouldn't
they go out dancing? And it actually probably was
only dancing, and if it wasn't, so what? Why
shouldn't he? What is wrong about that?"

"You know something, you're hypnotized
by bad behavior. You think it's stylish."

"Please answer me. I'm telling you what he

says. Just tell me what's wrong with that. That's his position."

"You say, 'I don't know what's wrong with that—it's probably great, but I don't want it.' "

"Do I then say, 'Look, I don't care what your needs are, I want you to stay at home. And not leave me to go out with strange women'?"

"That's right."

" 'I don't care if you're frustrated and wasted. You just stay at home.' "

"There's another way of doing it, of course."

"What's that?"

"It's called going back to the lawyer. It's called getting a divorce so he can go off and dance his fucking heart out every night of the week, only without humiliating you."

"I have this fantasy every other day."

"You are too young to be afraid to leave."

"Why am I so afraid? It's not because I don't want to."

"You *do* want to. That's why you're afraid."

"If I'd said that I want to come—I didn't actually want to go—but I had the chance of saying I want to come."

"Why should you? 'I want to come too.' No. What are you, an extra child?"

"He was trying to persuade all of us to go, and all of us were saying no, no, no. That girl wouldn't look me in the eye when she left. She said goodbye to everybody except me. So she knew it wasn't right."

"He's tamed you again. You were out of his control about three or four months ago, but he's tamed you again."

"Why can't it just get better?"

"It never gets better. It's like a play. They never get better, either. If you want to leave at the interval of a play, leave, because it's not going to get any better."

"But I don't know what I want."

"I've already told you a hundred times. You don't want to be in this mess. And that's why you have been marginally farting around with me."

"It's true that that's what made me feel free to, as you put it, fart around with you."

"Marginally."

"When we met, when I said to you I want distraction, that's what my motive was. And it was."

"Well, you've had the distraction, for whatever it's been worth, and now you have progressed to the next step. It always comes after distraction. It's known as taking your life in hand."

"I *could* go to a lawyer again. And the more predatory the better."

"Since I happen not to be in your husband's shoes, I agree."

"But what they would then get up to against

me—and I say 'they' because it wouldn't be just him, it would be him and his huge mother."

"Who's not so nuts about you to begin with."

"Well, she's not only that, she's vicious. She isn't just a miserable spouse, she's naturally vicious. And she's absolutely obsessed with her grandchild. She said to me the other day, 'You do realize that people can sue for access to their grandchildren.' "

"You should have kicked her right in the ass."

"It isn't my way."

"But it is your way to go to a lawyer again; that fits in exactly with your logical mind and your realism."

"Yes, but why am I so paralyzed?"

"You're terrified."

"I'm not terrified of him."

"No, of being alone and penniless."

"Why shouldn't someone be terrified, someone who's seen in her own family what I have? I have seen financial insecurity and I have been *marked* by it. Do you still think it would help to see a psychoanalyst? Because what I don't know is what I want."

"So you say and say."

"And he has a big hang-up about sexual power, my husband. It's a real problem. That's why it went—because of his obsession with sexual power. Looking around at what you might call all our middle-class friends, they accept the limitations of their sex life."

"He doesn't want to accept it."

"Well, I did."

"Some few do."

"He's so strange."

"He sounds rather typical to me."

"A typical man?"

"No, typical of a man like himself. Penetrate and withdraw. Penetrate and withdraw. He may be extraordinary in some ways but he's not strange."

"Why are all these friends relatively content while I'm so miserable?"

"How do you know they're content? You don't know anything until you see the position of their feet in the bed."

"Thank you, doctor."

"I'm not your doctor. I'm your friend. Your admirer."

"You see, it's been a difficult time for you to come back here and visit. I should have warned you."

"I would have come anyway."

*

"I went down for the weekend to see my mother, who's much better. But I sat there as if

anesthetized. As if someone had injected me with
some—some aging drug. You know, something
that will take the spirit out of you. Even she com-
mented on it. I just didn't do anything. My God,
I've been through so much with that woman, terrible things that I've handled, years and years of
ghastliness which I've managed to deal with since
my father's death. And she finally seemed so much
better and I was miserable."

"When the patient recovers the nurse falls
ill."

"Yeah, something of that. I remember
thinking that in order for me and my sisters to be
sane, it's essential for her spirit to be broken and
for her to be written off. I remember thinking it's
a family conspiracy. My uncles and aunts felt the
same: she's got to go."

"Those are ghastly feelings."

"With all the weight of difficulties I'm con-
tending with here, then to go down there—and
always to go down there by myself. I don't like that
because I know my husband is having a good time
in London, and it's painful that he won't come,
that a certain kind of decency is dead, that he
ought to support me more in it in a conventional
way. Sitting there with my mother I felt as though
I were waiting to die. She was in good form, she
was doing well, and she was getting me down so
terribly. Sometimes when one's in a bad situation,

life seems over and you're just waiting for the
time to be used up. Did you ever have that
feeling?"

"Sure."

"With your father?"

"No, not with him. My old father still lives
at the boil. He's got an opinion about everything
and often it's not mine. I sometimes have to suppress being a fourteen-year-old with my father.
Rather than waiting to die, sitting with my father I
sometimes feel as though I'm waiting for life to
begin. This last summer he got all riled up when
one of my brother's kids decided to marry a Puerto
Rican. Since he can't hide his feelings and usually
doesn't try, he got the kid riled up, and then my
brother got angry and he called me, and so I got
into the car and drove down from Connecticut to
New Jersey. When I got there he started in with
me about it. I listened for about half an hour and
then I said that maybe he needed a little history
lesson. I said, '*Your* father, at the turn of the century, had three choices. One, he could have stayed
in Jewish Galicia with Grandma. And had he
stayed, what would have happened? To him, to
her, to you, me, Sandy, mother—to all of us?
Okay, that's number one: ashes, all of us. Number
two. He could have gone to Palestine. You and
Sandy would have fought the Arabs in 1948 and
even if one or the other of you didn't actually get

killed, somebody would have lost a finger, an arm,
a foot, for sure. In 1967, I would have fought in the
Six Day War, and at the least have caught a little
shrapnel. Let's say in the head, losing the sight in
one eye. In Lebanon your two grandchildren would
have fought and, well, to be conservative, let's as-
sume only one of them got killed. That's Palestine.
The third choice he had was to come to America.
Which he did. And the worst thing that can happen
in America? Your grandson marries a Puerto
Rican. You live in Poland and take the consequences of being a Polish Jew, or you live in Israel
and take the consequences of being an Israeli Jew,
or you live in America and take the consequences
of being an American Jew. Tell me which you prefer. Tell me, Herm.' 'Okay,' he said, 'you're right
—you win! I'll shut up!' I was delighted. I had him
outfoxed and wouldn't let him go either, not quite
yet. 'And now you know what I'm going to do?' I
said. 'I'm going out to Brooklyn to talk to the girl's
mother. I'm sure she's down crying on her knees
too, giving her rosary beads a real workout. I'm
going out to Brooklyn to tell her the same goddamn
thing I told you. "You want to live in Puerto Rico,
your daughter marries a nice Puerto Rican boy all
right, but you all have to live in Puerto Rico. You
want to live in Brooklyn, the worst that happens is
that your daughter marries a Jew, but you get to
live in Brooklyn. Take your choice." ' Well, this

starts my father right up again. 'What kind of com-
parison is that? What do you mean, "the worst that
can happen"? The woman ought to be tickled to
death who her daughter's marrying.' 'Sure,' I said,
'she is—tickled to death just about as much as you
are.' "

"How did it end? What happened?"

"The marriage took place in St. Patrick's
Cathedral. With a rabbi in attendance. Just to be
sure they didn't try to slip us a fast one."

"What a carry-on! Why do they all magnify
these things so much?"

"Why do you all try to minimize them so
much? In England, whenever I'm in a public
place, a restaurant, a party, the theater, and someone happens to mention the word 'Jew,' I notice
that the voice always drops just a little."

"Does it really?"

"The way most people say 'shit' in public,
you all say 'Jew.' Jews included."

"I really think that only you would notice a
thing like that."

"That doesn't mean it isn't so."

"God, you are your father's son, aren't
you?"

"Whose should I be instead?"

"Well, it's just all a bit of a surprise, after
reading your books."

"Is it? Read 'em again."

*

"Why does everybody around here hate Israel so much? Can you explain that to me? I have
an argument every time I go out now. And I come
home in a fury and can't sleep all night. I am allied, in one way or another, with the planet's two
greatest scourges, Israel and America. Let's grant
that Israel is a terrible country—"

"But I won't."

"But let's grant it. Still, there are many
countries that are far more terrible. Yet the hostility to Israel is almost universal among the people I
meet."

"I have never been able to understand it
myself. It seems to me one of the most curious
freaks of modern history. Because it's just an arti-
cle of faith among left and left of center, isn't it?"

"But why?"

"I simply don't understand it."

"Do you ever ask people?"

"Yes, often."

"And what do they say? Because of the way
they treat Arabs. That is the greatest crime in all
of human history."

"Oh, sure, that's what they say. I don't believe a word of it. I think it's one of the most extraordinary pieces of hypocrisy in human history."

"Do they know Arabs?"

"Of course they don't. In English high culture, you could say it's because of this Foreign
Office fantasy about Arabs, and Lawrence of Ara-
bia, all this, coupled with a serious knowledge of
Arab interests, and families with all sorts of con-
tacts with sheikhs and who still get watches for
Christmas and all that rubbish. It's a kind of feudal
thing which the British quite like. You know, our
boys and their boys. But that's sort of establish-
ment—the actual antagonism comes from the so-
called intelligentsia of this country."

"And what do you think is at the root of it?"

"I don't think it's anti-Semitism."

"No?"

"Not in the main, no. It's just the fashion-
able left. They're very depressing. I can only come
to the conclusion that some people are so wedded
to certain unrealistic ideas of human justice and
human rights that they can't make concessions to
necessity of any kind. In other words, if you're an
Israeli you must live by the highest standards and
therefore you can't do anything really, just go back
and turn the other cheek, like J.C. said. But also
it seems to me an unspoken corollary that you criticize most harshly the people who actually behave
best, or the least badly. It's quite banal, isn't it?
These hotheaded people disapprove selectively
and most strongly of the least reprehensible
things. It's just unreal, isn't it? I think it has to do

with the last gasp of romantic hatred of the twentieth century. But it's not really as strong in this country as you may think."

"You think not."

"I'm sure not."

"Well, I'd feel much better if that's true. About this country, and about you too."

Laughter.

"I'm not anti-Israel. I loathe Arabs. We had them crapping on the pavement around our house, putting up property prices, and all the rest of it, the way the Jews would never do."

"We never crap on pavements. Putting property prices up is something else."

"Well, I think the Israelis have got into a very, very difficult position, and there's nothing really they can do, and they could be a lot nastier than they are. I think there are lots of reprehensible incidents, some of which we hear about. But that's the nature of the game. Look what happens in Northern Ireland. The torture of some particular individual, the shelling of a particular family of small children—nobody wishes as a matter of policy for disgusting incidents to take place. But perhaps they don't always regret them as much as they should."

"I never hear about Northern Ireland when I'm out on the town here. I hear only about Nazi Israel and Fascist America."

"Well, you don't hear that from me. People in this country who have any sense at all, who are people of any kind of discrimination and judgment, are not anti-Israel and don't believe that America is the Great Satan."

"These are people on the right."

"I would think on the whole they tend to be. Centrist types too."

"Is that what you are?"

"I'm nothing. I don't know anything about politics. Though certainly I know all the opinions. As if *everyone* doesn't know every last argument on either side of every issue and has to hear them again and again and again."

"That happened last night—some genius 'batting on,' as you say, about the sainted Sandinistas. And about the torture chambers the U.S. supports in El Salvador, Chile, and Guatemala. Supported by '*your* president,' he told me, 'by *your* tax dollars.' I said that I had no brief to make for El Salvador, Chile, and Guatemala, let alone for 'my' president, but since he was listing Latin American regimes which brutally crush any dissenting voice, I wonder how he could fail to mention Cuba. I said that because it is not a regime supported by the U.S., that doesn't make life any more pleasant for those who are imprisoned and tortured there. 'Cuba is strongly allied to Nicaragua,' I said. 'I would go so far as to say that this alliance goes unquestioned by the Cuban and Nicaraguan people, and unchallenged by the press that's permitted in both countries, whereas the alliance between Chile and us is openly attacked by opposition politicians, journalists, and academics in Fascist America. But leaving these differences aside,' I said, 'do you feel it is as reprehensible for Nicaragua to be allied to a country where people are imprisoned and tortured for their ideas as it is for the U.S. to be allied to such a country?' "

"And?"

"What do you think? 'Your president is going to blow up the world! What are *you* doing to stop him? What about your blacks? What are *you* doing for your blacks?' "

"Where were you having dinner, in a preschool nursery?"

"No, no, London's highest literary circles, my dear. Over dessert I defended dropping the bomb on Hiroshima *and* Nagasaki."

"You took that bait, *too?*"

"I defended Harry Truman against war crimes charges until one a.m."

"*Why?*"

"Because being a Jew and being an American in this country of yours is making me into a very contentious fellow. I'd forgotten about both, really. Then I moved to England and started attending smart dinner parties."

"I'M having trouble with the tenants —I think they're taking drugs.' 'Do you want me to come?' I ask. 'No. I have a friend staying with me. Andrew. It's okay.' She meets me at the airport. I bring her a Laura Ashley dress. Perfume. She kisses me tenderly. There's dinner for me. Then the door opens by itself. A six-foot black man. Shoes for two hundred dollars. A gold ring. A gold necklace. 'This is Andrew.' 'What is the function of Andrew?' 'Can he live in the spare room? He has nowhere to go.' 'I don't think there is any future together here with Andrew. He can go to a thirty-nine-dollar motel.' 'You think Andrew could have dinner?' 'It's my first night back, but okay.' If he was white I would have said no, but you can't tell a black person, straight into his nose, no, you can't have dinner here. Then I see some of my condoms are missing. Olina is having trouble with the IUD and I am using condoms. We're going to the theater. 'Can Andrew come with us?' 'Do you think he'd enjoy it?' I ask. 'He's half illiterate.' He comes to the theater. I notice at the theater that she's leaning toward him. I separate them and pull her to me. Coming home I start speaking in Czech. I say, 'Listen, this Andrew has to leave the house.' She says, 'It's very impolite to speak Czech.' 'He's a tenant—fuck it.' To Andrew I say, 'You have to leave tomorrow.' He comes down the next day and tells me, 'You pushed a button too much.' She says, 'I love him. I want to marry him.' To have someone fucking in your bed for four weeks! And to have my Olina lying into my eyes! I was close to buying a shotgun. Not a rifle but a shotgun. Wait for the man and shoot him into the trousers. I had a mild heart attack. Terrible chest pains and I'm in the hospital for a week. My lawyer laughs. 'You have a joint account with your wife?' But I trusted her as a Czech girl, not

as an American bitch. It's that nigger that does it.
I don't say 'black person,' I say 'nigger.' This girl,
educated in a Catholic family, she was frigid. She
went to bed with me in a long nightdress. Never
had an orgasm. I'm not so young but I used to be
a very good worker. Unfortunately, I never got
anywhere. Impossible. But he gives her an orgasm
on his black prick. It wouldn't be hard to give
Olina something to smoke and then stick it in. A
real Slavonic character is Olina. He's a typical
pimp type. An unsuccessful operator. Has a four-
thousand-dollar Hasselblad camera, a truck—and
that's it. Has nothing. Does little odd jobs. Doesn't
know how to spell, writes like a child. This half-
illiterate black guy lives with that beautiful girl in
a motel about thirty miles from the center of the
city. In one room with a shower, in a motel. Black
guy doesn't work. Lives off her unemployment
benefits. She was fired. The productivity of her
work dropped because all the ladies took part in
the soap opera of her life. She cried a lot and they
fired her. She looks bloody awful. She suffers a
great deal. She wants to divorce me because she
says that she loves that man. You know how
women are. Suddenly she felt the terrible desire to
be somebody else. The speed with which this
gentle aristocratic Czech lady was pushing for a
divorce! A hard-hearted, proud person is Olina.
Good. Fine. I couldn't kiss ever again the mouth

that sucked that long black prick. Only she has too much love for that black guy. He's unable to take that, especially if there's no money forthcoming. He's too primitive. He doesn't understand it. He'll leave her. She will return to Prague because she will have nowhere else to go. But this is the Soviet Union she will be dealing with, not a washed-up old emigré like me—never again will she be able to go to America. Authorities will always be worried that she is a spy. All because of his long black prick! He did not fuck her the way you fucked her, for her stories. He fucked her for fucking. You are more interested in listening than in fucking, and Olina is not that interesting to listen to. She is even less interesting to listen to than to fuck."

"I never fucked Olina."

"You're lying to me, my friend."

"She's lying to you, if it's she who told you."

"You fucked her four times. In New York. When we were all such good friends after I arrived from Prague."

"Not even once, Ivan."

"Other men listen patiently as part of the seduction leading up to the fuck. That is why men usually talk to women—to get them in bed. *You* get them in bed to talk to them. Other men let them begin their story, then when they believe they have been sufficiently attentive, they gently press the moving mouth down on the erection. Olina told me about you. She repeated it a couple of times. She said, 'Why does he keep asking these irritating questions? It is not emotionally conventional to ask so many questions. Do all Americans do this?' "

"Ivan, enough of whatever this is. None of it is true."

"With the nigger it's his prick and with the Jew it's his questions. You are a treacherous bastard who cannot resist a narrative even from the wife of his refugee friend. The stronger the narrative impulse in her, the more captivated you are. And all of this, I must tell you, limits you not only as a friend but as a novelist."

"So my books stink too."

"Play dumb if you like, but you know the truth. You only enter into life to keep the conversation going. Even sex is really at the edge. You are not driven by eros—you are not driven by anything. Only by this boyish curiosity. Only by this gee-whiz naïveté. Here are people—women—who do not live life as material but live it soulfully. And for you the more soulful the better. You like it best when they are in posttraumatic shock trying to recover their lives, like Olina fresh from Prague. You like it best when these soulful women can't actually tell their own tales but struggle for access

to their story. That is the erotica of it for you. The
exotica too. Every woman a fuck, every fuck a
Scheherazade. They have not been able to gain
access to their story and in the telling of their story
there is a kind of compulsion to complete the life
—and there is much pathos in this. Of course it is
stirring; just the wash of their sound, the quality
of intimate conversation, to you is stirring. What
is stirring is not necessarily in the stories but in
their urge to *make* the stories. The undeveloped-
ness, the unplottedness, what is merely latent,
that is actuality, you are right. Life before the narrative takes over *is* life. They try to fill with their
words the enormous chasm between the act itself
and the narrativizing of it. And you listen and rush
to write it down and then you ruin it with your
rotten fictionalizing."

"How so exactly?"

"Yes, you *would* expect me to help you perfect your lousy art, you *would* want to talk about
literature, you shitface, after having helped yourself to my wife!"

"Cast it in the form of an insult if that
makes it more fun. In your eyes, as a writer, what
do I do wrong? Tell me. You've never wanted to
before and you know how much I respect your
taste. I've picked up a lot from the talks we've
had."

"You insist on playing dumb. Even *this* you

banally fictionalize. You are not even sweating. Maybe you should have been a wonderful actor instead of a terrible novelist who will never understand the power of a narrative that *remains* latent. You don't know how to leave *anything* alone. Just to give voice to the woman is never enough for you. You will not just drown in her cuntliness. You must always submerge and distort her in your hero's stupid, artificial *plot*."

"So that's my vice and ruination—blatant instead of latent. The blatant American. Look—listen to me, *please:* the reason I'm not sweating is because none of this is so. I'm an *awful* actor. When I'm guilty I can outsweat Nixon. Believe me, either it's your paranoia or Olina's vindictiveness that's convinced you I fucked her. You're the ones who, if I·may say so, are banally, blatantly fictionalizing. Her leaving you like this is obviously killing you. It's awful. I know how much you've lost already. Things haven't worked out for you here professionally—and now this, losing her. But don't extend your sense of betrayal to me. It's not justified. I hate to remind you, but I've been one of your supporters here."

"You were staring at her ever since the first time we all met."

"She's very beautiful, she's young, so I stared. But staring isn't fucking in my book."

"So why my Olina now tells me that four

times you fucked her is only vindictively to drive me even more insane."

"Something like that seems to be happening, yes."

"You shitface! You lying, pampered American shitface!"

"Calm down—*sit* down! You're going to give yourself another heart attack—and there is no reason for it."

"Don't worry, don't worry, little American boy, I'm not going to shoot a shotgun into your trousers."

"Good, because there's no cause to."

"No, you I'll shoot into the ears!"

"THIS is the situation. Zuckerman, my character, dies. His young biographer is having lunch with somebody, and he's talking about his difficulties getting started with the book. He's found a tremendous lack of objectivity in people's responses to Zuckerman. Everybody gives him a different story. There are two nightmares for a biographer, he says. One is that everybody gives you the same story, and the other is that everybody

gives you a different story. If everybody gives you
the same story, then the subject has made himself
into a myth, he's rigidified himself, but you can
sort of crack at it with an ice pick and break it
down. It's much harder when everybody gives you
a different story. You may be closer that way to a
portrait of a multiple personality, but it's also aw-
fully confusing. All right. You be the biographer
and I'll be the friend. The biographer is still at the
point, after having done a lot of research, where
he's not even sure he wants to go through with it.
Do I want to write this life? What's the real interest
in this life? He doesn't just want to retell the story
of Zuckerman's boring Newark. What interests
him is the terrible ambiguity of the 'I,' the way a
writer makes a myth of himself and, particularly,
why. What started it? Where do they come from,
all these improvisations on a self? By now the biographer is already somewhat angry with Zuckerman
and is trying to overcome it."

"Why is he angry with him?"

"Because of his sense of insignificance and
having to establish himself in relation to the subject. He's begun to turn against Zuckerman, to
resent him, because he has this responsibility to
him. We all need a mode in which to write—this
biographer seems to need either hostility or awe,
and so he oscillates from one to the other. He was,
in fact, moved by wading through all the childhood

stuff. You're back thirty-five years and the writer is unguarded by any sense of self-consciousness. He's not writing for any audience. It's the writer before the audience sets in. You see this slightly repulsive embryonic writer in his letters, trying out on one or two people, and in private, the voice with which he's going to try to capture the attention of the larger audience. And all the false steps. The falseness in the voice moves you more than anything else. You see the writer becoming more and more manipulative, slier and craftier and underhanded. Now this biographer—you—he's already written the biography of E. I. Lonoff. He wouldn't have undertaken Zuckerman's biography, but since Zuckerman only lived to be forty-four, he figures he can do it in two years. Lonoff drove him nuts. Lonoff destroyed everything, and it took him five years to do a hundred and eighty-five pages. None of the people in Lonoff's life would give him anything. Zuckerman died suddenly and so he didn't have a chance to destroy anything. The Lonoff book turned out to be a critical biography, *Between Worlds, The Life of E. I. Lonoff*. The tentative title of the Zuckerman book is *Improvisations on a Self*, and he started off thinking it was going to be easy. People say to him, 'Why are you wasting your time on a minor writer?' But he knows he's going to make money on this book. There's a lot of curiosity about Zuckerman. The fucking particularly. People want to know the dirt. It's going to be Book-of-the-Month Club. First serial rights to *Vanity Fair*. His wife, too, thinks he ought to be doing a major writer, but he says to her, 'We want to have a baby, we need a bigger apartment. I can do Zuckerman in two years. I need a hundred thousand bucks if we're going to buy a bigger co-op and there's no other writer I can do this fast for that kind of dough. He was forty-four years old, only four books, and the literary criticism isn't that difficult. It's the dream biography—the author died young, he led a juicy life with lots of women, he outraged popular opinion, he had an instant audience, and he made a lot of money. Also, he's a serious writer whose books are readable and I can go to town on the autobiographical issue. It's really the biography every biographer wants to write because the *issue* is biography. I wasted five fucking years on E. I. Lonoff and in the end I came up with his critical biography and nobody read it. It won some obscure prize.' 'But ten years from now,' the wife says, 'nobody's even going to read Zuckerman's books.' 'That's right,' he says, 'the only book they're going to read is mine.' "

"And what is it you expect me to do?"

"Play reality shift."

"Must I? I almost think I'd rather fuck."

"Please, I'm stuck. Help me."

"Oh, okay."

"You're the biographer. *You're* stuck. You're flooded by now with impressions and information and you have no idea where to go. You've been following every lead, trying just to go with the tide, and you feel tremendously unbalanced. That's why you ask me to have lunch with you."

"Who are you?"

"I am myself."

"How—?"

"Don't ask me how. I'll worry about how."

"Is this really the book you want to be writing? Because it doesn't seem to me like a very good idea, to have, in the same narrative, you *and* Zuckerman—"

"Who knows? We'll find out. Look—we're at lunch. I say to you, 'But, Fred, Bill, Joe, whatever your name is, you met Zuckerman yourself. Start from there. During the Lonoff biography you saw him about five times.' "

" 'Three times. I have notes. At that point I liked him but he intimidated me.' "

"Good. 'How?' "

" 'He somehow made me feel like an earnest graduate student. And I'm not really earnest, though I do present myself in an earnest way.' "

" 'But *he* was earnest.' "

" 'Yeah, but I guess my earnestness brought out his sardonic side.' "

"Wonderful. I love you."

"No you don't—you love *this*."

" 'Did he talk to you about Lonoff?' "

" 'Yes. He was really cordial. He gave me his letters. I don't know if he gave me all of them —he probably didn't. Now I'll find out. He had some imagination for my difficulties.' "

" 'Which were?' "

" 'Writing about this absolutely private man. And he gave me some good advice about writing. He was very lucid about writing.' "

"Who are you talking about?"

"Guess."

" 'What did he say?' "

" 'Well, I was in a crazy state when I was working on that book. Can you imagine? Five years. And Hope Lonoff and the children wouldn't talk to me. Wouldn't *see* me. They suppress the story of his every human exchange as though this fastidious hunger artist, whose high and rigid principles denied him so much of the pleasure of appetite and elemental life, in secret had the remissive history of Jean Genet. It would have been comical, all their obstruction, if it hadn't made my life hell. The self-imprisoning scrupulosity, the block against contaminating experience that all but strangled his art they monumentalize into his pious memorial. All that timidity, disguised as "discretion," about a man's contradic-

---

tions and pagan urges. The fear of desanctification
and the dread of shame. As though it's *purity*
that's the heart of a writer's nature. Heaven help
such a writer! As though Joyce hadn't sniffed filth-
ily at Nora's underpants. As though in Dosto-
yevsky's soul, Svidrigailov never whispered.
Caprice is at the heart of a writer's nature. Explo-
ration, fixation, isolation, venom, fetishism, austerity, levity, perplexity, childishness, *et cetera*.
The nose in the seam of the undergarment—*that's*
the writer's nature. *Im*purity. But these Lonoffs—
such a suffocating investment in temperance, in
dignity, of all damn things. As though the man
wasn't an American novelist but was ambassador
to the Holy See! . . .' Isn't that enough for now?"

"Absolutely not. No! You're cookin'.
You're on fire! You're dazzling! Go on, go on."

"But that would not be my position at all, of
course. I'd *side* with the Lonoffs. I happen to believe *strongly* in privacy."

"Who cares? This is exquisite. *Go on.*"

" 'And then all the things that Lonoff himself destroyed. Lonoff was so paternal—I had to
work through all my father shit with him. My wife
wouldn't believe that. She kept telling me, "Come
on, just type it up and hand it in. What's your
problem?" I showed Zuckerman a chapter. I was
so embarrassed, because I hate to show people
things that are messy and unfinished. He read it

and he said, "It's all here somewhere. But there are two things you're really going to have to do here. You can't do it right away. You're going to have to put this away for a while." ' "

" 'What were the two things?' "

" 'He said, "You have to write and you have to think." ' "

" 'And that was helpful to you? You didn't know that?' "

" 'It was helpful. The most helpful things are the most obvious things. Coming from someone else and said in a certain tone. He sort of brought me back down to earth. You work on the life of Lonoff long enough and there's a sense of this rarefied being. A kind of piety crept into my approach, which I couldn't stand. And Zuckerman was great, because as a young man he'd had the same feelings. He was very funny about it. He gave me a sort of license to transgress. Zuckerman was the great sanctioner. Not that I wanted to slash Lonoff to pieces. But I had to feel that I *wasn't* an earnest graduate student, that I *didn't* have to have this phony nobility I had about Lonoff, revering him and so on. Zuckerman told me how, when he visited Lonoff in his early twenties, Lonoff had said to him, "You're not so nice as you look." Zuckerman said to me, "I'm going to repeat to you what Lonoff said to me." And it was the most liberating thing he could have told me.' "

" 'How so?' "

" 'It liberated me from my scruples.' "

"Oh, sweetheart—why do you look so sad saying that?"

"Because *you* have no scruples and I just know what I'm in for."

"I have no scruples but I do love you terribly."

"You only do if I play reality shift."

"You were wonderful. *You* should be the writer, you know."

"Nope. Never. Couldn't."

"Why not?"

"Not a bad enough fellow. Insufficiently aggressive. Insufficiently ruthless. Insufficiently capricious, venomous, childish, *et cetera*. My scruples."

"But maybe you're not as nice as you look either."

"I'm afraid I am. It's grotesque. I'm English. I'm even nicer."

*

"I had a little adventure on Sunday. I was walking in Chelsea with my Israeli friend Aharon Appelfeld and his son Itzak. We were just off St. Leonard's Terrace, heading up toward the King's Road. We were on the left side of the street and coming along on the right side were two men in their thirties or early forties, who looked like professional men, nicely dressed in sweaters and slacks, out for a stroll. As they were approaching us, they began to cross over to our side of the street and I noticed that one of them, wearing a green sweater, was mumbling out loud, or repeating something out loud, and all the while glaring at me. I couldn't make out what he was saying—he was sort of half saying it to himself—but he kept it up even as they passed us and continued down the street. I turned to look after them just as he happened to turn to look after us, and he was still at it. I couldn't figure it out exactly, though I had a hunch. I shouted at him, 'What's bothering you?' At first he just glared back at me. Then he gestured at his own clothes and he shouted, 'You don't even dress right!' I got confused by that. My pullover sweater happened to be dark brown while his was green, but otherwise we were dressed almost exactly alike. Though I did have my beard, of course, and it is getting scruffy and needs a trim. So—what he'd seen, you see, was a bearded, spectacled, darkish man dressed more or less like himself, talking animatedly to a smallish, bald middle-aged man wearing a sports jacket and a sport shirt and to a dark-haired boy of eighteen, both of whom had been listening and laughing as they all three walked along the quiet, civilized streets of Chelsea on a beautiful Sunday afternoon at the end of the summer almost, I might add, as though they owned the place. He answered, 'You don't even dress right,' and just stood there glaring at me, full of fury. And then I knew for sure what it was. I could have killed him. If I'd had a gun I would have shot him. Not because I was that enraged for myself—it was because who I happened to be walking with was a dear friend whose mother had been killed by the Nazis and who had himself spent part of his childhood in a concentration camp. I thought, 'No, this won't do,' and I walked a couple of steps toward him and, in my best American accent, I said, 'Why don't you go fuck yourself?' He looked back at me for a second or two, but then he just turned and stormed away. I have to tell you, if there was going to be a brawl, I was counting very heavily on Itzak, Aharon's son, a big strong boy who does lots of push-ups every morning, but it turned out that the English gentleman wasn't looking for a fight. He was just furious, that's all, the mere *sight* of me on the quiet, civilized streets of Chelsea had simply driven him up the wall. The fury was in his stride, on his face, it was in every breath he drew. The whole thing left me very agitated—and a little puzzled. I couldn't understand what he'd meant by telling me that I wasn't even dressed right. Aharon couldn't figure it out either and Itzak was just amused. He's an

Israeli-born kid and he'd never actually witnessed
an anti-Semitic incident before. To this boy from
Jerusalem the man had just seemed ludicrous. But
I come from Newark and I kept puzzling over the
damn thing, and then it dawned on me: the reason
my clothes just like his were wrong was *because*
they were just like his. What with my beard and
my looks and my gesticulations, I should have
been wearing a caftan and a black felt hat. I should
have been wrapped in a prayer shawl. I shouldn't
have been in clothes like his *at all*. Well, that
afternoon Aharon took the train back to Oxford,
where he was staying with Itzak, and that evening
we had a few people over for dinner and I told
them this story. I was still full of what had happened and also I thought that his remark about my
clothes was kind of interesting for having seemed,
at first, so enigmatic. Actually, to run into an anti-
Semite on a London street didn't seem to me so
amazing—that could happen anywhere. No, what
amazed me was that every last person at that dinner was convinced that I *hadn't* run into an anti-
Semite. They were all amused by me, by how I
had, characteristically, misconstrued the meaning
of his behavior. He was just eccentric, they told
me, crazy—'mad' is the euphemistic Englishism
—he was just some kind of lunatic, and the incident was utterly without meaning. Except for its
proving, once again, what a paranoid I am on this

subject. I said, 'But what activated his "mad-
ness"? What about me in particular set him off?'
But they all just laughed and explained to me again
how nuts I am and, I tell you, never have I felt
more misplaced in *any* country than I did listening
to all these intelligent and decent people going on
and on denying what was staring them right in the
face. I remember the first year I was here, I was
watching television one night and there was a commercial for little cigars, cigarillos, whatever
they're called. It showed the final moments of a
performance of a play featuring Dickens's Fagin, a
Fagin complete with the enormous hooked nose
and disheveled mop of greasy white hair. The cur-
tain comes down, Fagin takes his bows—and then
the actor is back in his dressing room, in front of
his mirror, pulling off the hooked nose and the ugly
wig and scrubbing himself back to normal with
cold cream. Underneath the makeup there is, lo
and behold, a fair-haired, handsome, youngish
middle-aged, rather upper-class English actor. To
relax after the performance he lights up one of
these little cigarillos, contentedly he puffs away at
it, talking about the flavor and the aroma and so
on, and then he leans very intimately into the camera and he holds up the cigarillo and suddenly, in
a thick, Faginy, Yiddish accent and with an insin-
uating leer on his face, he says, 'And, best of all,
they're *cheap*.' Well, being characteristically my-

self, I was a little taken aback by this. I happened
to be home alone at the time and since I felt the
urge, suddenly, to ask somebody a few questions
about this place where I was now trying to live in
peace, I telephoned an old friend of mine, an English Jew up in Hampstead and I said, 'Do you
know what I just saw on television?' But when I
told him, he laughed too. 'Don't worry,' he said to
me, 'you'll get used to it.' "

"You really are boiling, aren't you?"

"Well, the insinuation that *I'm* the one
who's behaving badly by taking exception to these
insults does piss me off a little, yes. 'Oh, why do
you Jews make such a fuss about being Jewish?'
But is it we who are making the fuss? Do you believe that too, my dear?"

"I wouldn't dare."

*

"You asked me what lay behind the British
distaste for Jews—those were your words. I think
actually it *is* snobbery. And I'll tell you what
makes me think so—because it's not felt about
those Jews who are part of the aristocratic es-
tablishment or upper-middle-class establish-
ment."

"But Jews have the same snobbery about
Jews themselves."

"Yes. But I'm just trying to explain something to you. That the general perception of Jews
is of, I think—this may not be right—I think it's
of Jews who are not like that, who haven't become
part of British culture in the sense that they have
been here for centuries, like the Waly-Cohens,
who are very rich—"

"So it's money."

"It is with the aristocracy generally. You
can't *be* upper class without money."

"If you make it through into the upper
class, then you are relieved of certain distasteful
stigmas."

"I'm trying to tell you something interesting
and you're being quite resentful."

"No I'm not. I'm not. I'm listening."

"They aren't just rich. These certain families, like the Samuelses and to a certain extent the
Sieffs and the Seligmanns and the Montefiores,
and plenty of others, they are not only acceptable,
they are smack in the middle of British culture:
they own land, they captain cricket teams, they
master the foxhounds, they get into the House of
Lords—you know, the whole bit. Just the same as
anybody else in that kind of way of life. What people hold against certain Jewish manifestations is
that these are downmarket carry-ons. This may

sound very stupid to you, but I'm sure if I put it better, and more subtly—"

"You're talking about ethnic behavior. It doesn't go here. But what about the Italians in London, the Italians, the Greeks—do their down-market carry-ons excite the same disgust?"

"No. Because Italians and Greeks aren't prominent in other ways in English life. There's no doubt about it, the Jews achieve in disproportion to their numbers and therefore they attract attention."

"Is that distasteful as well?"

"No, not in itself. But it makes people quite twitchy."

"So behaving upmarket isn't really more helpful, finally, than behaving downmarket, where a Jew is concerned. Unless he has ten million pounds and captains the cricket team, virtually *any* manifestation of social behavior on the part of the Jew is going to elicit an enormous amount of sensitivity. Make people 'twitchy.' "

"Well, no, I don't think that's true. People don't feel like that about them. If you look into certain worlds, if you look into the world of art dealing that is carried on by a collection of aristocratic Jewish owners—but this is clearly a dangerous subject with you. You are getting more and more resentful with every word I say, and so I am saying no more."

*

"Can you explain to the court why you hate women?"

"But I don't hate them."

"If you do not hate women, why have you defamed and denigrated them in your books? Why have you abused them in your work *and* in your life?"

"I have not abused them in either."

"We have heard testimony from expert witnesses, expert witnesses who have pointed to chapter and verse to support their every judgment. And yet you are trying, are you, to tell this court that these authorities with unimpeachable professional standards, testifying under oath in a court of law, are either mistaken or lying? May I ask you, sir— what have you ever done that has been of *service* to women?"

"And why do you, may I ask, take the depiction of one woman as a depiction of all women? Why do you imagine that your expert witnesses might not themselves be contradicted by a different gang of expert witnesses? Why—?"

"You are out of order! It is not for you to interrogate the court but to answer the questions of the court. You are charged with sexism, misogyny, woman abuse, slander of women, denigration of women, defamation of women, and ruthless se-

duction, crimes all carrying the most severe pen-
alties. People like you are not treated kindly if
found guilty, and for good reason. You are one with
the mass of men who have caused women great
suffering and extreme humiliation—humiliation
from which they are only now being delivered,
thanks to the untiring work of courts such as this
one. Why did you publish books that cause women
suffering? Didn't you think that those writings
could be used against us by our enemies?"

"I can only reply that this self-styled equal-
rights democracy of yours has aims and objectives
that are not mine as a writer."

"Please, the court is not eager to hear once
again a discussion of literature from you. The
women in your work are all vicious stereotypes.
Was *that* your aim as a writer?"

"Many people have read the work otherwise."

"Why did you portray Mrs. Portnoy as a
hysteric? Why did you portray Lucy Nelson as a
psychopath? Why did you portray Maureen Tar-
nopol as a liar and a cheat? Does this not defame
and denigrate women? Why do you depict women
as shrews, if not to malign them?"

"Why did Shakespeare? You refer to
women as though every woman is a person to be
extolled."

"You dare to compare yourself to Shakespeare?"

"I am only—"

"Next you will be comparing yourself to Margaret Atwood and Alice Walker! Let us go into your background. You were once a university professor."

"I was."

"As a university professor, you engaged in sexual practices with your female students."

"That humiliates women too?"

"Does it not? They were honored, were they, to be chosen? How many times did you forcibly induce your students to fornicate with you, a professor acting in loco parentis."

"There was no need to exert force."

"Only because of the power to influence and control implicit in the relationship."

"Of course there is the possibility of abuse —there as everywhere. On the other hand, you may do your own sex a disservice when you postulate intelligent young women as lacking the courage to be desirable—as having no aggression, no imagination, no daring, no adventurousness, and no perversity. For an education in the temptation to brutal sensuality that springs up spontaneously between youth and maturity, for a lesson on the torrents of feeling that flow just the other side of the taboo, you might do well to study the erotic liaisons depicted by a French writer named Colette."

"A counterrevolutionary voluptuary named

Colette! A traitor bent on pleasure named Colette! How many students did you abuse and exploit in this way?"

"Three. I had love affairs, over the years, with three—"

"First you patronize us with a lecture on literature; now are we to have a lecture on *love?* From *you?* Be careful, sir, how far you go with your insulting ironies. The court may feel obliged to have patience with such behavior but, I must warn you, the vast, indignant television audience that watches these trials is not bound by the legal niceties that obtain here. You were an adulterer, were you not?"

"Still am."

"With the wives of friends?"

"Sometimes. More often with the wives of strangers, like you."

"And with whom was the treachery more perversely enjoyable? Whom did you delight most in sadistically betraying, friends whose wives you ruthlessly seduced or strangers whose wives you ruthlessly seduced?"

"Oh, you *are* a wonderful girl! You *are* clever! You *are* beautiful!"

"Your Honor, I must ask the court to instruct this *man* that I am not a 'girl'!"

"Come over here, prosecutor, would you please—"

"Your Honor, I *beg* you, the defendant is *blatantly*—"

"I want to ask your expert opinion about this—this—"

"Help, help, he's exploiting me, he's degrading me, he's defaming me, he's attempting with this grotesque display of phallic—"

"You delicious, brilliant, lovely—"

"He's maligning me, Your Honor—in a court of law!"

"No, no, this is fucking, sweetheart—I'm fucking you in a court of law."

"Your Honor, the television—this is pornography!"

"MY mother's a very smart, foxy woman, who did very well for herself, in what she wanted to do. Wealthy marriages. I guess she wanted me to follow in her footsteps. I didn't fall into that mold, I haven't lived up to her expectations. It's just as simple as that, really. I would call her a typically smart Jewish girl who came from a very coarse background of immigrant stock. As she said, she always had her eye on the ball, which was money. She made her trade-offs, which were considerable. And she settled herself first in England, which was a disaster. She didn't fit in with the English at all. Among other things, her table manners were bad, she didn't have the breeding. She married a man from a very wealthy English Jewish background. She was married to him for about five years. It started out as a loving marriage but it disintegrated very quickly. Her in-laws were very averse to his marrying a poor Jewish girl."

"Your father. Where'd she meet *him?*"

"He was married five times. He always married ladies. My mother was the exception. He always married genteel women who couldn't fight back. He was very good at spending money himself. He didn't want to work. He had some money from his family. His father was a very stern WASP lawyer and used to ask him every day, 'What have you done to justify your existence?' He left St. Louis, rejected everything that his father stood for, and came East. To tell you the truth, I don't know very much about him. He disappeared when I was about one. But I know that he was a very, very shrewd guy. That marriage sounds as though it was totally loveless, the whole thing. Each was sizing up the other for how much money do you have. My stepfather was like having a grandfather. When he died, he was nearly ninety. He was very sweet, but it wasn't a father, it wasn't the real thing."

"What was he like?"

"He met this woman—while he was married to his first wife—who was really no more than a high-class prostitute. She finagled a meeting in Central Park on horseback. He always regretted that. He said, 'If I hadn't been on my goddamn horse I would have saved a lot of money.' And a lot of heartache. She came after him full-scale. She was a lot younger and she said, 'I don't want to remain your mistress, I want to be married.' And his wife offered him to come back. She said, 'I'll take you back, Bernard,' but he said no, he'd made up his mind. And then on the honeymoon cruise, she would leave him in the stateroom and was slipping into other men's rooms. Every tutor that came in for the kids would become her lover. The humiliation was horrendous, and he was a gentleman of the old school. Yale graduate, revered surgeon. He'd never encountered anything like that in his life before, and it devastated him. Also, she tried to kill him in his sleep—she drugged him and she tried to hold a pillow over his head. She was a criminal."

"What happened?"

"She's in a madhouse now."

"How did he get rid of her?"

"Divorced her. All in the papers. Aerial views of the house. Big scandal. Terrible. They never forgot it in Bedford. They were always suspicious of my mother. What was this nice, intelligent man doing with another vulgar self-seeker? They thought she was a replacement, another facsimile of her. But he didn't know how to cope with someone like this. She'd come from Akron, the first destroyer, very bloozy and blowsy and feisty, and there was no way he could cope with her."

"How come you never told me all this?"

"I wanted to forget about my money-mad mother. I wanted to forget my missing father. I didn't want to carry on, like the college girls in the dormitory, endlessly and boringly about my family. I was above that. I wanted to carry on endlessly about 'The Blood of the Walsungs' and 'Michael Kohlhaas' and 'In the Ravine.' "

"And how are you now? How are you? What's been the fate of the smartest girl in the seminar?"

"I can't seem to communicate to people, that's how I am."

"You?"

"It's very frightening to me but I don't seem to remember the past. I really only vaguely remember you. I had shock therapy but that made it worse. That's when I was in the first hospital, about eight treatments. It was very pleasant, actually. They give you sodium pentothal. You're out. You don't know anything. After you come around you just feel groggy. They stopped giving them to me because they really didn't do that much. About twice a week. I wasn't frightened. I thought it was the answer. What I'm waiting for to happen is some kind of energy to come back. That's what's frightening. I just don't feel it. I try to remember things but I can only remember part of them. It comes back at times, but it's very frightening. You don't know what's going on. Things don't penetrate too much. I want so much to talk to people but I can't seem to do it. When I speak to people it's kind of a downer not to be able to talk to anyone, or answer anyone's questions, or use anything. I have to make a tremendous effort —like right now, with you. I don't know how to get around it, though. I feel so damn uncomfortable around people. I guess most of my life I've felt terrible around people. Excuse me, Philip, do you have an ashtray?"

"Are you on drugs?"

"Because I was so depressed they gave me a combination of drugs. They said there would be no problem with that, and that in the past the two drugs never worked against each other. What happened is that I had a very bad reaction. I became extremely paranoid. I had to be hospitalized. And I was going crazy. I really went off the wall. When they took me down for the tests I thought they were taking me to a torture chamber. I still swear to God that someone came into my room, and they had a paper, and they said, 'Will you please sign this paper that says you beat your mother to death.' I went into fits. 'How can you ask me to sign such a paper—how dare you!' Well, none of this, I'm told, happened. I swore to God that it happened, I really believed it. The doctor said they'd never seen such a reaction. That was in September. And I'm on an antipsychotic drug right now. To prevent a paranoid experience. I don't take as much as they want me to take but I take a fair amount. I mean I'm down to quite a little. Though sometimes I still get very afraid in crowds."

"But what did you in like this? How can this be? You were fine when I knew you. Intellectually stubborn and very shrewd-looking and boldly aloof for a kid, and you had great flair in those uncompromising black outfits. Very Hamletish. Beautifully imperfect too, with the student pallor and that chipped tooth and those tired eyes. Or does all that now sound to you like a description of your burden?"

"That's what you said to me ten years ago. The first time you took me to dinner in that restaurant on Third Avenue. Le Moal."

"I remember the dinner but not what we said."

"You wished me luck. You said I'd need it."

"Why?"

"Because some people might find me irresistible. I was so wild with nerves it was one of the few things I even heard. *That* I remember."

"I wasn't too calm myself."

"I couldn't have known that then. You were my teacher."

"That's why I wasn't too calm. You were something, silently slinking into class with all that disheveled hair and then laying down the law on Kafka. I remember those A students all reading Kafka's *Letter to His Father* and explaining exactly how 'Metamorphosis' and *The Trial* derived from his relationship to his father. 'No,' you said wearily, 'it's just the other way around. His idea of his relationship to his father derives from 'Metamorphosis' and *The Trial*.' Set them up with that and then delivered your haymaker. 'By the time a novelist worth his salt is thirty-six, he's no longer translating experience into a fable—he's imposing his fable onto experience.' Not too many nineteen-year-olds say such things, not within my hearing, anyway. Elegant performances given by you in that class. You were already somebody."

"Was I already crazy?"

"No. No. No, absolutely not. Don't you impose a fable on *your* experience. High-strung, of course, but to me you seemed astonishingly *poised*."

"Maybe you were also crazy."

"And maybe I wasn't. You wrote me a note, in that first class of mine you took. 'I pray for only one thing every night, and that is to be a good writer.' "

"Is that how the little vixen went about it?"

"It was young—so what? You *were* young. But that note was you: direct and straight. Tell me again what happened. What did this to you? Make me understand the shock treatments and the hospitals. I just can't."

"The old old story—deceived by life. I had a fatal attraction to hypnotic womanizers and I went batty."

"Is that an accusation?"

"Only if you feel like taking it as one. No, with you it was fresh—so fresh I was hypnotized by *me*. There I was, on weekends, still snuggling up in my Doctor Dentons under the covers in my bedroom in Bedford, with my ballet shoes in the closet from when I was ten, and then, Monday afternoons, total abandon in some anonymous bed in some anonymous room on some anonymous floor in some anonymous Hilton. And so intimate, it made my head spin—the only familiar thing in that entire hotel was our flesh. I suppose you *could* call it basic training. And it *was* scary. For months I went sleepless. When you said 'love' it gave me terrible gastritis. But it was exciting, all right. The fatherly lover who listened. Somebody who is dis-

illusioned involved with somebody who is innocent
—educational all around. At least nobody in that
Hilton was into murder."

"You fell for the boys who shoot to kill."

"Yes, sex merchants, basically. The libido
mob. Couldn't resist them. Didn't know how to flirt
with them. Didn't know how to handle them at all.
That's something we failed to cover in that seminar. And, of course, I was catnip for the ones who
wanted me who I didn't want. What was driving
me crazy was that there was always somebody running after me passionately, calling me up on the
phone, and coming after me, and swamping me
with invitations; you know—drowning me, basically. And at the same time there was the absentee
lover, who was gone and not interested, or playing
a lot of games with me, and I went a little bit crazy,
kind of nuts. It happens. It was all right at the
beginning, but the mistake was that it happened
over and over and over and I couldn't seem to get
out of it. And that's been my nemesis. That's been
the whole thing."

"Didn't you have any affairs that weren't
fraught—that were pleasant?"

"Sort of."

"What happened to those?"

"I got bored."

"**I'M** much fatter."

"A bit. Not quite the matron yet."

"I was even fatter. I've started to lose it."

"What is it, a protest you're making against something?"

"I don't worry about anything anymore. I'm not anxious anymore."

"Since I disappeared."

"I don't know what it's since. But I think what keeps me thin is undue anxiety."

"And how's that go down on the home front —does he like 'em nice and fat? I like 'em the way you used to be, thin and neurotic."

"Well, things are much better. I don't know how permanent it is. But what happened since you've been gone was a shift in the balance of power. In my favor. And it's been very slow and painful. It was very bad up until three weeks ago, but he's just slowly begun to behave much better to me. Don't ask me why. But I can't spend the whole rest of my life being so bored, apart from everything else. I go into a panic about it which ends with making an appointment with a good solicitor. It seems to me that I keep going into rehearsals. Very tiring. You don't know if this is going to be just a dreary pattern, just a little marital misery that you go through from time to time, or whether, on the other hand, they are steps into the abyss, the kind you study about in history. What happens in history is that it's dotted with disasters, and when you study history, you go from one disaster and you look forward to the next, and you have steps into the abyss, and there are dates and concepts, you learn those, and then you pass the exam. The trouble with life is you don't really know if this is a downward process. The trouble with life is you don't really know what's going on at all."

*

"'How do you know such things? You've never been here before. How come you think you know about these things?' And I said, 'What the hell are you talking about? I've been thinking about these things for twenty years. I've been thinking about these things for as long as I could think. Why shouldn't I know about them? And, what's more, I thought I was here to talk. Why shouldn't I have some views on it?' They said, well, that's fine, but why shouldn't I be nervous for a year?—that's the message, that you sit around being timorous. And I said, 'I *am* nervous. I don't want to expose myself,' and then they said, 'Well, we're angry with you about that as well.'"

"What is this 'we'—they take a vote?"

"No, that is burlesque. But it comes out very clearly. They are a little family and I'm the new girl. And they're not sure they want a new mate in the family."

"And it's all so transparent?"

"Yeah. Crass. So I got very angry, and then one of them said something really silly. 'I can warm to Wilfred, I'm sure if I could understand his vulnerability I'd learn to love him, but I can't figure out his vulnerability, so I can't care for him.' And I said, 'Are you suggesting, is it an assumption of yours, that if you spot someone's vulnerability you ipso facto care for them?'—I didn't say 'ipso facto'—and she said, 'Well, yes. Why do you want to know?' And I said, 'Well, I'm just curious to know what the assumptions are around here. Because that's why I've had difficulty talking about myself. Because I don't know what you all think and how it all works and so forth.' At this point, the analyst, who's very sensible, chipped in and did support me, but they were angry with me yet again. She said, 'But what's wrong?' And I said, 'Look, at the worst extreme, this kind of language, which covers up certain kinds of assumptions, is nothing but psychobabble.' 'Are you accusing us of psychobabble, blah blah blah?'"

"How many are there?"

"Eight to ten. They're supposedly professional people. It makes me angry. I just have gone six or seven times. I'm not going again. It's worth it to me as copy—I like to hear them talk about themselves. But they're angry with me because I'm too clever. It did give me the most wonderful charge, this group, for about a month. One is even a novelist. Well, would-be sort of. A woman. She was the one who I had most to learn from, who was most interesting, and who most disliked me. She was most articulate, she spoke beautifully, it was fun to listen to her, and she couldn't bear somebody else also speaking well. It's stupid of her because the way she speaks well is quite different from the way I do. There's this solicitor fellow called Wilfred. There is a guy who works for the

Festival Hall. There's a woman who has a lot of expensive jewelry and a Louis Vuitton bag, which means—"

"She doesn't know anything."

"Yes. What else? At least two of them were training to be psychotherapists."

"The first day you must have been nervous."

"I wasn't at all nervous."

"And you got into the room and there they all were and you said, 'Hello, I'm the new girl.'"

"No, no. I was the first there. They all turn up late. They're all just awful. It's just like being late for family dinner. They all sort of trickle in. And they spend an awful lot of time staring at the floor not saying anything. Which given that it's quite expensive is quite annoying. I don't know what they think they're doing. And a lot of them clearly make sacrifices to go."

"What was your maiden speech?"

"I don't remember. But it was probably a sort of well-disposed sensible question. I always knew what they were going to say in the end, but I thought I better not let on to that, so I just asked leading questions, like a barrister. Obviously somebody felt that she never got any attention in life and this is why everything was so unfair and horrible, and so I said, 'Are you the only child in the family?' These are the kind of acceptable questions. And this can get on to whether or not you're used to dividing attention. But they're hopeless. They don't get anywhere. I felt like saying I don't think they can deal with any real problem that I might have, I don't think they have the sense to do it."

"But aren't they supposed to deal with the problem of you and not with your problems?"

"I suppose. Who knows? I thought it would make me understand in practice why relations at work are so difficult and why I hate my job so, a crappy job with stupid people ordering me about. Somebody in this group started accusing me of thinking I was a clever girl. And that's exactly a problem I have. And I was longing to hear more about all that. Although I find it hurtful as well."

"But you *are* a clever girl. I love you for being a clever girl. Where's the problem? Who are these people? I'll go over and punch 'em all right in the nose."

"Of course they're going to be envious because I *am* cleverer than them and what the *fuck* are they going to do about it? You know the conclusion I came to?"

"What?"

"I came to the conclusion that I ought to be more drastic."

*

"I've just seen my daughter performing in her Nativity play. The Nativity is something we have about the birth of Jesus."

"Is that what it is?"

"Yes."

"When did that happen? I probably was paying no attention. I missed the newspaper several days last week."

"Well, it was actually quite a long time ago. And they've read a lot into it. I wish you could have seen it. It was so funny. It really was funny. It was in the drawing room. With a grand piano and a marble fireplace. My daughter was so funny. She's such a little card. She was a queen, as in the king. She had to bring gifts. We got to talking about it one day and I said, 'What are the gifts?' and she said, 'Well, there's gold, fuckincense, and myrrh.'"

"Did you correct her?"

"I didn't, actually. I just said, 'Which are you giving?' and she said, 'I'm giving gold,' and I thought, 'Fine, she doesn't have to mention it probably.' I'm afraid I have to go back to this scene of Christian triumphalism quite soon."

*

"I'm going to have a birthday this year again."

"Not again."

"Yes. No way round it. Subtract nineteen thirty-three from nineteen eighty-four, and there's no way around it—it's fifty-one."

"Of course you could totally ignore it. Why do you take it so hard?"

"You, who's pissing and moaning about being thirty-four?"

"I know why *I* take it so hard. I'm asking why you take it so hard."

"Because life will be over soon, that's why. I'll be dead."

*

"One of the unfair things about adultery, when you compare the lover to the spouse, the lover is never seen in those awful dreary circumstances, arguing about the vegetables, or burning toast, or forgetting to ring up for something, or putting upon someone or being put upon. All that stuff, I think, people deliberately keep out of affairs. I'm generalizing from tiny, tiny experience, almost none. But I think they do. Because if they didn't it would be so unrestful. Unless you like two sets of domestic conflict, and you could go from one to the other."

"Yes, with the lover everyday life recedes. Emma Bovary disease. In the woman's first flush

of passion, every lover is Rodolphe. The lover who
makes her cry to herself, 'I have a lover! I have a
lover!' 'A kind of permanent seduction,' Flaubert
calls it."

"My handbook, that book."

"What's your favorite part?"

"Oh, the brutal stuff, of course. When she
runs to Rodolphe in the end for the money, when
she pleads for three thousand francs to save her
and he says, 'I haven't got it, dear lady.'"

"You should read a little aloud to your
daughter each night at bedtime. Flaubert's a good
girls' guide to men."

"'I haven't got it, dear lady.' Delicious."

"I used to tell my students that you don't
need three men to go through what she does. One
will usually fill the bill, as Rodolphe, then Léon,
then Charles Bovary. First the rapture and the
passion. All the voluptuous sins of the flesh. In his
bondage. Swept away. After the torrid scene up at
his château, combing your hair with his comb—
and so on. Unbearable love with the perfect man
who does everything beautifully. Then, with time,
the fantastical lover erodes into the workaday
lover, the practical lover—becomes a Léon, a rube
after all. The tyranny of the actual begins."

"What's a rube?"

"A hick. A provincial. Sweet enough, attractive enough, but not exactly a man of valor,

sublime in all things and knowing all. A little foolish, you know. A little flawed. A little stupid. Still
ardent, sometimes charming, but, if the truth be
known, in his soul a bit of a clerk. And then, with
marriage or without—though marriage will always
speed things along—he who was a Rodolphe and
has become Léon is transformed into Bovary. He
puts on weight. He cleans his teeth with his
tongue. He makes gulping sounds when he swal-
lows his soup. He's clumsy, he's ignorant, he's
coarse, even his back is irritating to look at. This
merely gets on your nerves at first; in the end it
drives you nuts. The prince who saved you from
your boring existence is now the slob at the core of
the boring existence. Dull, dull, dull. And then the
catastrophe. Somehow or other, whatever his
work, he fucks up colossally on the job. Like poor
Charles with Hippolyte. He sets out to do the
equivalent of removing a bunion and gives somebody gangrene. The once perfect man is a despic-
able failure. You could kill him. Actuality has
triumphed over the dream."

"And which are you to me, do you think?"

"At this moment? I'd say somewhere between a Rodolphe and a Léon. And slipping. No?
On the slide to Bovary."

"Yes." Laughing. "That's just about right."

"Yes, somewhere between desire and dis-
illusionment on the long plummet to death."

*

"I've never seen such a thoroughgoing ex-
ploitation of sado-masochism in my life. Bacon's
portraits look like nothing so much as what you
want to do to your enemy."

"How dramatic."

"But there are people, aren't there, who
you don't actually want to do violence to—you just
want to smear their faces like paint."

"You're more aggressive than I am."

*

"Why do all these Slavs come to see you?"

"Czechs aren't Slavs."

"Well, why do you see all these Czechs and
Slavs?"

"Why they come to me and why I see them
are different questions."

"Why do you see them?"

"I like them."

"Better than the English."

"Wouldn't you?"

"Why? Because they suffer so much? Are
you *that* in love with suffering?"

"I'm interested in it. Isn't everyone?"

"Hardly. Most people prefer to avert their
gaze."

"Well, I'm counterphobic and I stare. Displaced persons have things to tell you. Sometimes you can even lend a hand."

"A soft spot for victims—is that from being Jewish too?"

"Is it? There are plenty of Jews who couldn't care less. I don't think of myself as a Jewish victim, you know. Quite the contrary."

"But that's it, though—you're of the little pocket of Jews born in this century who miraculously escaped the horror, who somehow have lived unharmed in an amazing moment of affluence and security. So those who didn't escape, Jewish or not, have this fascination for you."

"They hold no fascination for you?"

"I'm curious, but I don't go out of my way to cultivate them. I would never think of going to any of those countries for a holiday, while spending two weeks in a place where everybody is oppressed and miserable is your idea of a good time. How did you get onto that?"

"It was accidental. I'd finished a book and I was traveling. It was '71. We drove from Vienna to Prague. After just the first half hour of walking around that place, I thought, 'There's something here for me.' I had a publisher there, who'd published my first book years before. I went to the publishing house the next morning and introduced myself and the director and his staff toasted me with slivovitz at ten a.m. Then I went to lunch with one of the editors, who told me that the director was a swine. I began to get the idea. A thousand stories later I was there alone for a few weeks one spring and I got corralled on the street by the police. Over the years I'd got used, each spring, to being followed everywhere by the cops, especially when I went to see writer friends, but these were polite plainclothesmen who kept their distance. This time—it was '75—two police in uniforms came directly up to me on the street and asked to see my papers. I showed them my passport, my visa, my hotel identification card, but they said that wasn't enough, I had to come with them to the police station. I began to shout, alternately in English and in my high school French, that I wanted to see the ambassador at the American Embassy. I was only a few feet from the trolley stop and I started shouting at the people standing there that I was being harassed for no reason by the police and I demanded to be taken to the American Embassy. One of the cops meanwhile went up the street and there was my plainclothesman, in his blue raincoat, and the two of them talked for a while, and then the uniformed cop came back and said I had to go to the police station—he spoke in Czech, but I got his drift all right. I still refused to move and just kept shouting. This went on for about fifteen minutes. Each time I said no the cop

would go back up to the plainclothesman for in-
structions and then come back and insist that I
had to go to the station. A young German couple by
the trolley stop had come up close to see what was
happening. They spoke English to me, and I said,
'Will you stay here until this is settled?' I told them
my name and where I was staying and to call the
American ambassador if I got dragged away.
Eventually the cops got so frustrated that they *both*
went up to the end of the block to talk to the plainclothesman. Just then a trolley pulled up at the
stop. I thought, 'Why wait to be arrested?' I
hopped on the trolley and it started away. I was in
a terrific sweat by then and my heart was pound-
ing, and two stops down I jumped off the trolley
and ran across a bridge and got a trolley going in
the opposite direction. I took it to God knows
where and jumped off next when I saw a phone
kiosk. I telephoned one of my Czech friends and
told him what had happened. He laughed. He said,
'They only wanted to harass you. They only
wanted to scare you.' I allowed as though they had.
He assured me that nothing further would happen
to me if I went back to my hotel—and I went back
and nothing did. Except that after that I was never
able to get a visa to Czechoslovakia again. The
evening after I left Prague, they picked up my
friend, the one I'd phoned, took him from his
house, and questioned him all night at the police

station. He wrote later to tell me that all they
wanted to talk about was me and my annual visits.
They kept asking him, 'Why does he come to
Czechoslovakia all the time?' And he said, 'Haven't
you read his book? If you read more, you would
know. He comes to Czechoslovakia for the
girls.' "

"And is that so?"

"No. I went to Czechoslovakia for the
jokes. I come to England for the girls."

*

"Everyone I keep meeting these days—I
remember you at Oxford, they say, you wore transparent blouses and no bra on."

"So you're an ex-extrovert."

"Yes! And it's all true. Everybody used to
disapprove of me because I had my hair dyed red
and exposed my breasts."

"Well. I haven't seen your breasts exposed
around here for a long time."

"That's true. But I'm not friends with them
anymore."

*

"Do you think I overestimate you?"
"No."

"You think I have you right."

"Well, I am clever. I have no sense of intellectual fashion but I'm still quite clever."

"So what do you think I should write about, if you're so clever?"

"Not me."

*

"You've come for your lesson."

"Yep."

"Did you do your homework?"

"I'm not sure."

"Okay. Let's lock up here before we start any of that stuff."

*

"I'd rather you didn't call me anything today. The nameless one."

"How about Nobody?"

"No, that's too definite."

"If you called a character Nobody, I wonder where it would land you. There was a character called Nobody."

"I would think you'd need more ideas than that to begin a book."

"That's more than I usually begin with. No-

body went to Heathrow Airport. Nobody boarded
a plane. Where did Nobody go?"

"Nobody went to France. Why did Nobody
go to France?"

"Because Nobody likes it."

"Then Nobody meets Somebody. The other
character is Somebody. Nobody and Somebody
became lovers."

"And?"

*

"Let me give you a drink."

"I'd love a drink. I feel very much between
things."

"Which things?"

"You and the deep blue sea."

*

"You're looking very well. You're looking
quite different."

Laughs. "You always tell me that."

"What time do you have to get back to
work?"

"I think I should get back sometime in the
afternoon."

*

"That's one of the nicest things that's been done to me all week."

"I liked it too."

*

"He doesn't really understand why I don't do any work. But he's determined to think well of me and to like me. Because he's a nice man. The other day I was going to spend the entire day not working—I was going to come here as a matter of fact. I was going to spend the day behaving quite disgracefully. I said to him, 'I'll be gone all day, out of the office, mainly for the purposes of self-advancement.' And he was so upset. He wanted me to tell him a nice lie, you know. Can you imagine this man? He's very good-looking. And he's a Christian. He's a terribly decent man. He always has this slightly conciliatory, appeasing look. He knows that I behave so badly at work."

"Do you behave so badly?"

"Well, in a sense. I just pissed off today. I've done nothing since about half past twelve. And there are certainly things for me to do. I mean, by ordinary standards they are paying me to do some things. Do you ever feel like getting a job? It's very nice really, seeing all those people every day, and they all say wonderful things.

They're often very funny. You might actually enjoy it more than this."

*

"It's all very harassing—endless demanding phone calls, stupid domestic chores, and boring people who give you a hard time to work with if you just show them a single weakness."
"You look so fucking tired."
"I know. But what can I *do?*"
"I don't know, sweetheart. Run away."

*

"There's something in this cigarette."   .
"Yes."
"Somebody slipped me a Mickey."
"Uh-huh. Me too.
"You're slightly swimming."
"I'm slightly sinking."
"Swimming before my eyes."

*

"You're very official today."
"I'm in a terrible mood. I'm feeling terrible at the moment."
"Well, at least you haven't lost your looks."

"Haven't I?"

"Nope. The fight's still in you."

"It comes and goes."

"When the fight's still in you, you look pretty good."

"It's funny, that sensation that you're losing it, it's very odd."

"Losing what, the fight or the looks?"

"Both. I think they're all connected."

"You mustn't lose the fight."

"It's not entirely in one's control, I don't think."

*

"You might not think so, but I really did do some quite remarkable things as a teenager, things which were very unusual. The last thing I did, being Mummy's good girl, was to get all those scholarships when I was sixteen to Oxford and Cambridge. Most people can't get them at eighteen. And it was English, which is the most difficult subject because there are thousands and thousands of applicants. Anyway, it just *was* clever. Or, at any rate, somehow this performance could be forced out of me. Actually I enjoyed that, I enjoyed those exams—I could do all those things, I was good at them. That's what's perplexing me so about now. Why do I find it so difficult *now?*"

"Why *do* you?"

"I guess because so much of my married life has been so bad for me. I just operate on one cylinder these days, as opposed to three or four, or however many other people have functioning. Even a small thing, like doing something slightly difficult rather well for only a few hours, has such a devastating effect upon my morale. It's really something, when I think of myself at sixteen."

*

"Why don't you step over here and give me a kiss?"

"I don't want to. I'm not feeling at all good. I'm not feeling terribly communicative. I've had enough of this new shrink. I don't think this stuff is for me. Actually I think they're all quite creepy. I think they perv off a bit on—"

"Perv off?"

"Oh, awful schoolgirl slang. I think they take a perverted interest in, and pleasure in— that's what it means. I'm not going there anymore. It upsets me too much, really."

"How many times did you see him, about ten?"

"About that."

"And when did you stop?"

"Today, actually. I just called up and canceled. I have to go to see him or write to him that I don't want to go."

"But why? Where was he leading you that you didn't like? Or did you just think that he was stupid?"

"I didn't think I'd heard anything that I hadn't thought of a million, million times before. Not one single thing that was new."

"What did he make of our deceiving your husband like this?"

"I never talk to him about you."

"Never? Then he wasn't getting the full story, was he, of these last four years?"

"You've simply distracted me from the central concerns of my life."

"Oh? I was *intended* as a distraction all right, but it didn't work out that way, you know. Because I became a temptation: a source of fantasy in the beginning, a source of possibility after that, and then, eventually, a disappointment."

"Is that how you see yourself?"

"In your life, yes. That's how I think you experience it."

"Why?"

"Why do you experience it that way or why do I think that?"

"Either. It's the same, actually. You can only tell me what you think; therefore whether you tell me the objective truth or what you think, it's all the same."

"But that *is* what happened to you. I saw you. I watched you. I saw the color in your face. I felt you tremble. You used to tremble when you came here, remember? Hide from the shrink whatever you like but that's what used to happen."

"He's not the kind of man you can tell anything to, really."

"Then he's really in the right job."

"He was awful. I'd tell my cleaning lady more than I'd tell him."

*

"You're looking kind of cheery, honey."

"I'm doing much better."

*

"How are you doing? You seem a bit sad."

"This little shit upset me. They're very good at upsetting people. A lot of them are really rather unpleasant. The unpleasant ones, who are always young men, very young men, they have a specialty—a lot of them are public school boys— they have a horrible line with women, particularly women who show any sign of hesitancy, they just like to tear into them."

"They tore into you."

"They would have. I walked out. I came here. Here I am again."

*

"I do have some kind of courage, which I'm always feeling myself lacking, because I've just had two perfectly ghastly nights. All-night rows."

"Why the hell are you still having these rows?"

"Because neither of us can accept what we recognize. Though sometimes it does seem that we're entering new territory, and we did seem to be, because he was actually talking about moving out. I was saying that would be quite a good idea. And he didn't like that very much, so . . . I mean all this kind of practical discussion seems slightly different from the mutual recrimination. But it does of course degenerate into a quarrel. But *I* can't move out. Because I would have to spend all my time trying to get injunctions to get him to pay the rent on whatever I'd found. I can in theory, but in practice, no. You see, as long as we're still fighting, I think he thinks if only he can get it right somehow, he can have everything, he can have his girlfriend, and the outdated wife . . . oh, it's all kind of hopelessly vague."

"We'll move on to another subject then."

"Please. Immediately."

*

"I listen to you a lot, you know."
"Too much. Why do you?"

*

"What is it?"
"I'm thinking that I still love you."
"Really? Despite?"
"Despite."

*

"It's beneath you to stay in a marriage because you think you can't get another job and this way you have a meal ticket."
"A meal ticket is not beneath anybody."
"It's beneath *you*."

*

"If the marriage is so clearly over, why don't you go? I no longer understand."
"I don't want to."
"There is your dignity, you know."
"That won't exist without an income."
"Clever but not true. Just the opposite is true."

*

"I have a check for you."

"That's terribly nice of you. It really is. But I can't take it."

"Why don't you just cash it? Put it in your bank. Hide it at your office. Just don't deposit it in your joint account."

"We don't have a joint account. He's not so foolish. It's terribly nice. Can I frame it?"

"No. And don't mislay it."

"Can I put it in my Bible?"

"No, you can put it in your bank for a rainy day."

"It's terribly nice of you."

"Why don't you think about it, before you throw it away? You can do whatever you like with it—just don't mislay it."

Sets it down. "Thank you very much."

"Well, it would be best if you took it."

*

"Either you're a guilty secret, which makes me deceitful in a very important argument in which I am demanding honesty and plain dealing. Or if things do degenerate, I think it'll be easier if it's true to say that I've had absolutely nothing to do with you for an extremely long time. And finally, if I end up living on my own, I ought to be emotionally freer than I am. With you."

"Okay. I will miss you. I'll miss you a lot."

"I'll often think about you too."

"It's a damn shame about you and me."

"Do you know that poem of Marvell's?"

"Which poem?"

"'It was begotten by desire upon impossibility.' That poem."

"I thought it was 'despair'—'begotten by despair.'"

"It is. It was. Both."

"HOW are you?"

"I'm all right. I'm about to go in today."

"I thought you would be. What do you know? Anything new?"

"No. I'm going to have a CAT scan this morning. It's quite a heavy day."

"I see. And the CAT scan will tell you what?"

"How much longer. No—if the CAT scan shows tumors, then it's all bad news, the drugs aren't working, and if it doesn't show anything, I still have to have surgery to see what's going on. They'll read it to me on Monday. And so . . . I don't know what to say. I feel all right. How are you?"

"I'm okay. So—this is a big weekend."

"It was all supposed to happen on Good Friday, but I thought that was loading the symbols."

"Yes, it's not good literature. It's not even good life."

"I don't know. Every time I do this I have to get this strength out of somewhere. It's like draining a swamp. I don't know where to get it. Maybe it's like the reverse of draining. What would it be? Making a swamp?"

"Are you able to write anything?"

"Not a lot. Narrative crumbles under the weight of these endless stories."

"You writing these endless stories down?"

"No, I'm not. I don't function from one sentence to the next. No, I've been doing yoga. Some macrobiotic. And I've just been trying to live with what joy there is. You know, this kind of indefiniteness is very disconcerting."

"How's your support system going?"

"Great. Even my father phoned from wherever the hell he lives now."

"So it's not so great."

"No, they *are* great. All my ex-men are being very nice. Look, just a *call* from my father makes cancer worth it. I could do with a hand from you, though. Are you ever coming back to America?"

"I'll be in New York in a month. I'll see you the day I get there."

"Good. What's up over there? What's your life in London like?"

"Not much different from what it was like when we were criminals on Eighty-first Street."

"Still writing, are you?"

"Yep."

"I thought you'd give that up, with any luck."

"No. In my room with my typewriter all day, and social and cultural events in the evening, and it's all opaque and English to me. I'm off to a cultural event tonight. I was to a social event last night."

"The social events are called dinner parties."

"Yes. The trouble with dinner parties is that I get seated next to other men's wives."

"Of course."

"You know something about other men's wives?"

"They're boring."

"They are not as interesting as you when you were another man's wife."

"Who was there?"

"Too boring."

"And where's my book?"

"What book?"

"The book with me in it. I like that one."

"My dear, you are going to have to do something interesting that I can stick in there."

"I am. I'm probably dying."

"You don't know that."

"I'll know Monday."

"I'll phone Monday to find out what the score is. What your score is—okay? Look, you'll find the strength somewhere. And now I'm going to stop before I utter still more platitudes."

"Yes, I know a platitude when I hear one."

"Me too. 'Bye."

"Goodbye."

*

"Hello."

Singingly. "Yes, hello."

"What's up?"

"Well—a miracle. Yeah, it's a miracle."

"Tell me about the miracle."

"It's a miracle. The CAT scan showed no trace of pathology. Which means that in three

months this thing that I was told was incredibly
virulent, and I had a thirty to fifty percent chance
of it being okay, and if it wasn't okay I'd be gone
within a year, seems to be responding at lickety-
split speed to this stuff. And the doctor's very
pleased and he seems to think that the prognosis
is now changed. So it's a fucking relief."

"Yeah, I'll say."

"Strange, very strange, because it's so fast.
There's not a trace of it. I still have to be opened
up in June to make sure that what the CAT scan
can see is the same as what you'd get from a test
tube inspection, but—you know, the thing could
recur but not with these drugs. I think at worst it
means that if I could have these drugs for the rest
of my life I could have a life. But they don't even
think that. They just think that I should finish this
course of treatment and then just hope that it
doesn't recur. It very often doesn't. I think everybody is very surprised. If you looked at my CAT
scan now and anybody else's, from that evidence I
have no longer got cancer. So it's amazing, eh?"

"Pretty good. You did all right."

"I did all right."

"Did you think you had it in you?"

"Noooooo."

"That's called a pardon from the governor."

"It certainly is."

"But who is the governor?"

"I don't know. But clearly I have to stay on his good side for a while. It doesn't mean that this is all a nightmare which is past. It just means that there is much pressure removed."

"Now the CAT scan, that's your entire body?"

"No, it goes from my groin to my heart. And the doctor said that if there was any tumor any-where else there would have been something, a fluid, a shadow, in that area, which is the area where it starts. There is this thing called the pre-ferred path of these cancers. You know about that?"

"That's in your notes, not mine."

"Well, the next place this thing would have gone is the liver. It doesn't go to the brain."

"The Preferred Path."

"Yeah. A title. But I'll wait on that, I think."

"Look, this is all terrific. I didn't know what I was going to hear when I phoned you. This is extraordinary news."

"Quite a day, though. I told them not to tell me but in fact the technician rushed out and told the person I was with that it was clean and there was nothing and it was all wonderful. That made me very nervous."

"Well, yes—your character hasn't changed in all this."

"I'm very happy that I haven't gone into a large depression. I thought there might be something hideous in my nature that would make me weep at the news."

"You're entitled to any reaction. There is no preferred path of emotion. This is great news. I'll just say goodbye to you then. There's nothing more to say, is there?"

"You mean, that's it?"

"Absolutely. Now that you're well . . . "

Laughing. "Exactly, I knew you'd feel like that. . . . No, I really don't think so. I think we must be friends again now, old friends. Anyway, I'm not completely out of the woods, so you can still be a little nice to me."

"And when you *are* completely out of the woods?"

"Then you can return to normal."

*

"I had such a lovely dream about you."

"You did, really?"

"I had the most wonderful dream about you. The essence of you, my dear."

"Speak a little louder."

"How can I speak louder? It's hard to say these things."

"Oh, so that's why your voice is so soft.

Well, pull yourself together and say them. You've been through worse. What happened to us in your dream? Anything that didn't in days of yore?"

"Oh, yes."

"Really? That *must* have been some dream. I was quite in love with you."

"Were you?"

"Oh, yes."

"Well, that helps. It's wonderful to hear your voice. I can't tell you how lovely this dream was, and I wish you'd had it too."

"Well, write it out and send it to me. I might be able to stick it in the book about you."

"Don't be silly. I'm not going to lay myself on the line."

"You sound shaky."

"I have chemotherapy today."

"That's why I called."

"Then I have this god-awful operation. And I just feel, because I feel fine and I'm getting on with my life, that they're going to give me some little yank back to the . . ."

"It's not going to happen."

"The aftereffects are pretty grim."

"As grim as when you began?"

"Much worse."

"Why does it get worse?"

"Because the poison's inside you."

"But by Sunday you're yourself?"

"Not really anymore. It takes till Tuesday or Wednesday."

"When do you leave the hospital?"

"Tomorrow morning. They just throw you out. Then I come home and I sleep for fourteen hours straight."

"And then on, say, Saturday how do you feel?"

"Like you have very bad flu. Up and in bed. Up and in bed. And then I get on with life, such as it is."

"And how do you look? Are you wan, are you thin?"

"I wish I were thin. I look bursting with health. And I have no hair. Otherwise I look great."

"You have no hair—you have a wig?"

"No, I don't have a wig. I have all these god-awful babushkas."

"The hair is going to grow back?"

"Yes, but it needs a little encouragement. It gets whapped once a month."

"Listen. You are feeling well and you are well-looking and those things must point to something."

"Yes, it points to the fact that I'm not going to go immediately. There's a possibility that there'll be tiny little cells still in there that the CAT scan didn't pick up. Unfortunately that'll mean another six months of this stuff. I'm dreading that. And of course the worst nightmare is that there's a surprise for the doctors when they open me up, and they see the whole thing is full of tumors."

"Can that possibly be?"

"I don't think so. But how could any of this possibly be?"

"No answer."

"I may be bald but I'm not even forty. I really don't think I should die."

"You won't."

"That's what you said in the dream too."

"Well, I can't be wrong twice in twenty-four hours."

"Say that again."

"I can't be wrong."

"Again."

"You're not going to die."

"One last time."

"You're not going to die. You're going to live."

"All right. Thank you. 'Bye."

"**WELL,** I've missed you too. I was thinking of coming over to see you, if you would see me."

"Oh, really? What about your lying? What about my being a guilty secret that keeps you from being honest?"

"Oh, well, I'm not sure."

"You're not sure about what?"

"I think I've been changing a lot."

"Are you learning to be a liar?"

"I wouldn't say that."

"Tell me the truth."

"What truth?"

"What are you trying to say?"

"I'm simply saying that I was thinking of coming round to see you."

"But you had all those principles about plain dealing."

"It's not a question of principles. It's a question of how relationships work. Isn't it?"

"I don't know. You tell me."

"Well, I think so. I think certain relationships . . . you know, you're not free to tell lies or conceal the truth—whatever the reasons, they're ultimately boring but they're there."

"But I thought you were not free to tell lies."

"That's right, that's what I thought I wasn't."

"Aren't you?"

"Well, I'm not so sure."

"I don't understand."

"Well, I don't really either. But I think I've been changing—I don't want to go into this."

"You might as well."

"No, no, I mustn't."

"Well, look, darling, of course I want to see you—but what have all these months without you been about then?"

"Well, you might well ask. I suppose I seem very capricious, or something. But probably I shouldn't come anyway."

"I think you wanted to try something. You tried it. I don't think you're capricious at all."

"I don't really want to talk about it. But it's not silly."

"What happens now? Are you bound to tell the truth?"

"Yes, and I'll bring a couple of gossip columnists and a fingerprint man."

"I'm confused."

"Yes. But I'm sure you've had relationships like this yourself, though, in which the balance of power changes radically for one reason or another. And the whole thing has changed."

"So what's happened? You better tell me."

"No, I don't want you ever again to be confused by my domestic life."

"I wasn't confused in the old days. I'm confused now."

"No, no, you shouldn't be confused now. You should just ignore the whole thing. Really, it would be much better. If I spend my entire time telling you about my domestic life and leaning on you and all that, it's hopeless."

"Is that what you were doing, leaning on me?"

"Yes."

"And now?"

"I don't want to lean on anybody, you know. Not because I disapprove of it or anything like that. Just because I'm like a tadpole whose legs are emerging. A tadpole of thirty-six. Sad, isn't it?"

"But if questioned under oath, what are you going to say?"

"What do you mean under oath? In court? Well, listen [*laughing*], I would not lie in court, I must admit."

"Then you oughtn't to come."

"I might lie in court in some circumstances. But not necessarily."

"Do we know what those circumstances are?"

"No."

"Then maybe you oughtn't come. I'd love to see you. I'm dying to see you. I'm really very confused by you at this moment."

"Sorry. I don't want to be tiresome."

"Don't be silly. But I'm telling you I'm confused by you. Of course I missed you. Terribly this afternoon, in fact."

"What do you miss?"

Laughter.

"Oh, come on. I don't want any dirty talk."

"I'm afraid some of it would be dirty talk."

"Well, I suppose that has its place."

"Yes, well, then come around. Sure, come around, my little liar."

"**ARE** you interested in politics because you're a Pole or because you're interested in politics?"

"I think mostly by being a Pole. It came from a feeling of being quite desperate about our situation. And finding ways to make it better. One has to get involved. I'm not very active in the underground—because I cannot find a place for myself. Because I'm not a Catholic and the Polish underground is mainly Catholic. I was born a Catholic but I'm no longer a Catholic. Even the Jews in the underground accept the Polish church, which I cannot do. Because I think they keep the Polish people with the mentality of the Middle Ages. And I think it's also because of the church that our situation is economically and politically what it is. It is a very backward force. Both my parents are long dead, long ago, and though they were born Catholics, they were not practicing. They sent me to have my first Communion."

"What are you, about thirty?"

"Me? Thirty-three. I left my faith in the secondary school. It didn't interest me anymore. It didn't give anything. No inspiration. It was just going to church and listening to sermons which were not inspiring."

"What do you remember about your childhood and adolescence?"

"My father suffered oppression—a lot. He was a director of a coal mine. In Silesia. Before the war—and after the war he had a lot of assets in this coal mine, and under the Communists, of course, he lost everything. And the Communists moved him to another position because he didn't want to join the Party. He died of a heart attack. I came to the university after '68. I was still in a secondary school when '68 happened. I studied English philology. Can you tell?"

"Yes. Oh, yes."

"English culture, English history, language, and so on and so forth. A very nice thing happened to me yesterday. A nasty thing happened before, then a nice one. It was rush hour. I went to Charing Cross station. Hundreds of people going past me, and I felt very unsecure. I bought the ticket. And then I couldn't find my way to the platform. I mean I knew where the platforms were but I couldn't find the right platform. I didn't know how people find out such things. I couldn't find any information center. I was lost in the crowd and people were in such a hurry. And I approached the gateman. He was barring the door because one train was leaving, and beside me was a very hysterical woman trying to get past the barrier, and he was trying to push her out. Somehow I managed to ask him humbly where the platform for Greenwich was and he said, 'Look at the board, lady.' And I thought, 'What kind of board? My God.' Then finally, yes, there was a board—there were all sorts of signs and I couldn't find the solution to the signs. Finally I calmed down a bit and found the right train, the right hour, and the platform. I was slightly relieved. But I am still in this terrible crowd—people were pushing me because I was standing in the middle of their way to the platform. And probably the panic must have been in my eyes, because I thought I behaved quite normally.

I kept walking to the platform and I showed the ticket to the man in the booth, who collects it or, I don't know, *checks* the ticket. And I showed it to him, then put it back in my purse, and he grabbed me—he leaned out of his booth and he grabbed me. And he shook me and said, 'Cheer up!' I was shocked."

"You must have looked terribly despondent. You must have been despondent about more than that."

"Yes. It was just terrible. But I loved this man. He was very nice. It never happened to me before that somebody reacted to me in this way. And one more thing happened to me, two hours before. I went up the escalator in one of the undergrounds, and many people went, and I wasn't in a hurry, and a lot of people were passing me. And I noticed a friend of mine passing me in a hurry, and before I managed to react—I hadn't seen the man for ten years—he was somewhere up the stairs where I couldn't catch him. I stood there looking."

"That happened earlier."

"Yes."

"So you were already upset and frustrated by this."

"Yes. Also. Things are strange."

"He was a Pole."

"No. He's American. He was my lover. Ten years ago." Laughing. "Imagine passing him."

"Your lover in America?"

"No. In Poland. He came to Poland, twice. He thought himself a poet and he wanted to find his 'roots.' "

"He was a Polish American?"

"No. An American Jew."

"You mean his Jewish roots?"

"Probably."

"So that did disturb you a little."

"It was so strange, don't you think?"

"Yes. On the other hand, you're like a tinderbox. You know what that means?"

"Uh-uh."

"It isn't hard to make you explode. Or go off. You happen to be suffering the human predicament times ten. Anybody who spends, as they say, two weeks in another town, is always a little susceptible but you're even more so. Here. *Tinder*. 'Any dry or flammable substance that readily takes fire from a spark and burns or smolders.' A tinderbox is a box containing tinder. Get it?"

"The tinderbox gets it, yes. At home I'm using the same dictionary. I use it for translation. It takes most of my time, translation. When I get back from the office, and take care of some house duties, and when I put my daughter to bed, I sit down to the translation. Three hours." Laughing. "To make my life more meaningful. I want to use my life properly, to some good cause."

"We all try to do that, you know. Even privileged Westerners."

"I got this strange thing that I knew you already when I met you two days ago at the party."

"Maybe we understand each other. However, yours is a different fate from mine. I don't envy you."

"Yes, the Communists want to make life easier for everybody, so that's why they torture us. That *is* different."

"What are you laughing at now?"

"At you, of course."

"Well, why not?"

"I have so little experience with Jewish people. I don't know anything about anti-Semitism. By the time I got around to being born, there were no more Jews left in my country. I couldn't even recognize a Jew. I wasn't aware of different facial characteristics. I don't know why. Because I read literature, I read descriptions, but somehow, no experience in the streets. It happened in Long Island the first time. My husband and I were a year in America, before we had my daughter. He was studying. We were on the train to Manhattan, and there were a lot of people going to work. And at one station the Jews got onto the train."

"How did you know that?"

"My husband said, 'Look, those people are

Jewish. If you want to know how Jews look like, look at them.' "

"They weren't religious Jews."

"No, no, no. Executives. With briefcases."

"Jews with briefcases."

"Yeah. Strange? No."

"No. Stranger today are Jews with side-locks. What did you see, aside from their brief-cases?"

"Hair like yours. Clothes like yours—no." Laughing. "Later on I started noticing the fea-tures."

"But you'd had this lover, searching for his roots. Didn't you take a good look at him?"

"He didn't look that Jewish. But now when I try to remember, yes, he did have some features. But it somehow didn't strike me as something dif-ferent. Look, I guess I must leave now."

Kisses her. She laughs. "What is it, senti-mentality?"

"No, just pity." Both laughing. "Anyway, I'm kissing your sentences, not you. I'm kissing your English."

"I kill you. I come here with a bomb."

"I'm like the Communists. I'm just trying to make your life easier."

"You're just trying to make my sentences more *complicated.*"

"Of course—also to find out why you go around spying on Jews."

"**YOU** better tell me what's upsetting you so. I cannot come home from my studio every day and sit down to dinners like this night after night. You don't speak. You don't respond to anything I say. And you look awful."

"I don't sleep."

"Why don't you? Tell me."

"I don't know."

"What's bothering you?"

"It's nothing to do with you."

"That's no reason not to tell me. It *does* have to do with me, doesn't it?"

"I want to know—no, I don't, I don't want to know!"

"Oh, here we go. What *is* it?"

"You do not go off to your studio to work—you go off to your studio to fuck! You are having an affair with someone in your studio!"

"Oh, do I? Am I?"

Bursting into tears. "Yes!"

"The only woman in my studio is the woman in my novel, unfortunately. It would be nicer with company but it doesn't work that way."

"Not your novel—your notebook! You left it out of your briefcase and I picked it up and stupidly—and now I wish I never had! I *knew* not to open that—I knew it would be awful!"

"You are working yourself into a state over nothing, you know."

"Am I?"

"Well, what do you think? You happen to have read some notes—"

"Not 'notes'—conversations with this woman!"

"Who is imaginary."

"How can she be imaginary when she knows all these things *you* couldn't possibly know? She is someone who comes to your studio and she

is why you have been so distracted and totally un-
interested in me now for months. When I speak to
you, you're barely able to stay awake. When *she*
speaks to you, it's all so wonderful that you have
to write it down, every wonderful word. She so
much as opens her *mouth* and you're an 'écouteur
—an audiophiliac.' God, what pretentious crap!"

"She could well be why I have been unin-
terested in everything for months—and then again
the book I'm writing may be why I have been interested in nothing else for months."

"You do—you do—" Crying bitterly.

"Do what?"

"You love her more than you ever loved
me!"

"Because she doesn't exist. If you didn't
exist I'd love you like that too. I can't believe that
we are having this argument."

"We're having it because you are lying!"

"Really, this is too stupid."

"I suppose talking to Rosalie Nichols in the
hospital was imaginary, too. But you *did* talk to
her in the hospital, you *told* me you talked to her
in the hospital!"

"I did. And wrote down some of what we
said to each other—and more that we didn't say I
made up, and where the real exchange ends and
the invented one begins I can't even remember
anymore. Her situation was awful, she was being

so gallant, and I didn't want to forget it. Some of what's there is accurate reporting and it inspires what I would hope is accurate imagining. My Czech friend Ivan, crazy as he may be, never accused me of sleeping with Olina; we had no such falling out after she left him—did you read that part?"

"I read it all! I already had on my coat and, *stupidly, stupidly*, I sat back down and read the whole thing! Oh, it's so much better *not* to know!"

"Well, I don't believe this soap opera, really. You must dramatize everything."

"It's you who dramatizes, who has to have this one because she's the voice of *Mitteleuropa* and that one because she sounds so fucking well born—"

"Look, this is simply too corny. I refuse to explain myself. I refuse to have this argument with you, of all people. I refuse to remind you that the sounds people make hold a certain appeal for me, and maybe this is a notebook about *that*. I have imagined a love affair—I do it all the time. Not the way most men ordinarily do, while clutching at their dicks, but because that is my *work*."

"But I've *read* those chapters, the manuscript chapters you gave me to read about the English woman—and this is *not* that English woman, this is the *model* for that woman, this is *the real woman!* Don't pretend they are one and the same!"

"I don't. One is a figure sketched in conversation in a notebook, the other is a major character entangled in the plot of an intricate book. I have been imagining myself, outside of my novel, having a love affair with a character inside my novel. If Tolstoy had imagined himself in love with Anna Karenina, had Hardy imagined himself in an affair with Tess—look, I follow my leads where they take me—ah, the hell with it. What do you propose, that I police myself? That I don't follow through on this sort of impulse for fear—for fear of *what?* Enlightened prurient opinion? Well, not by you and not by anyone will I be censored like that!"

"Oh, the self-righteousness of the liar caught with his pants down! Don't be so fucking self-righteous, and don't scream at me—I cannot be screamed at! You are caught and you are trying to confuse me!"

"I am trying to straighten you out! I gave you the example of Ivan and Olina. When Olina ran off with that black guy, we *did* have lunch together, Ivan and I, and he *did* tell me all about what had happened, but he did *not* go on to accuse me of having betrayed him with his wife. I never did betray him with his wife, never was accused of betraying him with his wife, *except in that notebook you read.* I portray myself as implicated because it is not enough just to be present. That's

183

not the way I go about it. To compromise some 'character' doesn't get me where I want to be. What heats things up is compromising me. It kind of makes the indictment juicier, besmirching myself. As is proved, if you still doubt me, by this fucking argument."

"But the Polish woman you *did* meet at Diana's party. You told me that. You had to tell me when she called you here."

"And? So?"

"You had an affair with her too."

"Did I? Too? She was only here a week."

"So—that week. You had to have an affair because of the overwhelming enchantment of her accent! And who is the little American loony? Where does *she* fit in?"

"Control yourself. *Think.*"

"*She* thinks—go argue with her!"

"Who is 'she' this time?"

Crying. "Your thirty-six-year-old."

"Let's get the notebook, okay? Let's sit down here and go over it. I will, if I have to, explain to you, line by line, if I have to, what I have been up to, as best I understand it. I will tell you which bits are out of conversations I have had with any number of people—including Rosalie Nichols and that Polish woman *and* 'the little American loony'—and those that are not, which happen to be the preponderance of what you read.

A lot goes back to the affair, before I ever met you, with Rosalie. When she turned up with her husband upstairs on Eighty-first Street, they were moving *from* England. Did it never occur to you that she might be the English woman whose England—*and* whose marriage—I was drawing on in what you read? Look, I don't mind your reading it. I wouldn't have left it lying around if I worried about your reading it. I carry it back and forth between here and the studio because sometimes I sit in the bedroom, as you know, sit in the bedroom chair at the end of the day, while you are asleep in bed, and make up little conversations between myself and this woman. And other women too. Maybe to the degree that I carry on like this in the bedroom where you are sleeping, maybe to that degree I am guilty of a sort of perverse betrayal. But then I am not the only man who thinks about imaginary women while in the bedroom with the woman he regularly sleeps with. There may even be women who behave just as impurely in their bedrooms with the men they regularly sleep with. The difference is that what I impurely imagine, I am impelled to develop and write down. A mitigating circumstance: my work, my livelihood. In my imagination I am unfaithful to everybody, by the way, not just to you. Look, think of it as an act of mourning, because it is that too—a lament of sorts for a life I did lead before you. I don't any longer,

I actually happen to live as married men were once
supposed to—but allow me to miss the old ways
just a little. Such longings aren't entirely unnatu-
ral, you know. Please, if coming upon my notebook
has caused you all this misery, I am sorry and I
wish it hadn't. But I do have to say, what you are
confronting me with is a naively perfect paranoid
misreading."

"So, except insofar as I'm supposed to believe that she's based on an English woman you
had an affair with in New York a hundred years
ago, she doesn't exist, other than in your imagination."

"And in yours."

"And you never had an affair with Olina.
I'm to believe that too. Otherwise I'm not only
paranoid but, even worse, philistinely naive."

"Ivan was broken enough, he'd lost enough
—Olina was all he had. Not only did I not but he
never even accused me of it. Nor did he ever tell
me what a lousy writer I am. Phone him in New
York and ask him. Phone Olina—ask *her*."

"Explain to me if you will, then, how you
happen to know all these things about English life
that this English woman who doesn't exist tells you
in your studio while you are conducting this affair
with her in your head."

"Because I've been living here awhile and I
sometimes pay attention. Because I learned a little

from Rosalie. Because it's my business to seem to know more than I do. This woman is simply the repository of all that.''

"But the conversations are so *intimate*."

"I see where that might be maddening. Of course I understand how this might drive you just a little nuts. But intimacy is interesting too—it's a subject too."

"Postcoital intimacy. That's the subject."

"Is it? I hadn't thought of it precisely that way."

"Well, please do. That serenity. That talk. That's the whole mood. You're more intimate with her than you are with me."

"That isn't true."

"Lately it is."

"Well, these things wax and wane—detachment and tenderness, incredible tenderness and then incredible inaccessibility, that's the pattern with people who've stuck together as long as we have. What I'm thinking about with her isn't that. It's the love that exists *because* it's compartmentalized. The stolen moment that can't be sustained."

"It's sustained in that notebook."

"You know, I ought really to interpret your jealousy as a terrific tribute to my persuasiveness."

"And I suppose I ought to interpret what

I've read here as a measure of my terrific failure. Whether I believe she exists or whether I believe she doesn't exist, certainly the love for her exists, the desire for her *to* exist exists. And that is even more wounding. The whole notebook is nothing more than an attempt to escape the marriage and me."

"And if it were? If it is? Where have *you* been? The attempt to escape the marriage is an ingredient of marriage. In some I've seen it's the vital principle that keeps it going. I wrote these things out, not to wound *you*, but partly, I think, to trace down the logic of that—the *illogic* of that. It's too bad you can't read it that way."

"How would you read it if *I* was charged up with desire for somebody who is everything *you're* not?"

"You really cannot allow yourself to be crushed like this over a situation that is invented."

"Can't I? Can't I? Oh, you're right. It isn't fair, I'm sure. It's just, you have been so remote . . . terribly remote."

"If so, that's something else."

"No, no. It's the same thing. You wouldn't have an imaginary friend, you wouldn't need an imaginary friend . . . And are you going to publish that notebook? The novel and then the notebook, the tragic lament for the life you once led? Is that the plan?"

"I don't know."

"Don't you? Is that why the sections are interspliced like that, with all that Czechoslovak mirroring of everything, because you don't know?"

"It's occurred to me. I'm not sure what it adds up to, if anything. But of course I've thought of it."

"To publish it as it is?"

"I said I don't know. There's something to be said for being shed of all the expository fat, but I haven't begun to think it through. I don't really know what it is I've got. A portrait of what? Up till now I have been fiddling with it on the side and mostly worrying about the novel."

"Well, maybe you should, you know, think it through. Because what you've got a portrait of is adulterous love, and, consequently, it might be advisable to take your name out—don't you think? 'Philip, do you have an ashtray?' You would change that to 'Nathan,' would you not? If it were ever to be published?"

"Would I? No. It's not Nathan Zuckerman—it's not meant to be Zuckerman. The *novel* is Zuckerman. The notebook is me."

"You just told me it's not you."

"No, I told you it is me, imagining. It's the story of an *imagination* in love."

"But if one day it should be published more

or less as it is, liberated from exposition et cetera, people aren't going to know that it's just a little story of an imagination in love, any more than I did."

"They generally don't, so what difference does that make? I write fiction and I'm told it's autobiography, I write autobiography and I'm told it's fiction, so since I'm so dim and they're so smart, let *them* decide what it is or it isn't."

"Yes, I can see where that might be a lot of fun for you and your readers, letting them decide —but what about me?"

"You'll have to decide as well, if you insist on not believing what this actually is."

"I meant, what about humiliating me?"

"How could you be humiliated by something that's *not so?* It is *not* myself. It is *far* from myself—it's play, it's a game, it is an *impersonation* of myself! Me *ventriloquizing* myself. Or maybe it's more easily grasped the other way around—everything here is falsified *except* me. Maybe it's *both*. But both ways or either way, what it adds up to, honey, is *homo ludens!*"

"But who would know that, aside from us?"

"Look, I cannot and do not live in the world of discretion, not as a writer, anyway. I would prefer to, I assure you—it would make life easier. But discretion is, unfortunately, not for novelists. Neither is shame. *Feeling* shame is automatic in me, inescapable, it may even be *good;* it's yielding to shame that's the serious crime."

"But who is even talking about shame? All it would require is your having that wretched American girl say, '*Nathan,* do you have an ashtray?' All it would require is that, in three or four places, and none of this would be a problem for anyone. Where are you going?"

"Out! Somebody telling me what to write happens to drive me absolutely nuts, so I am going out!"

"Don't. Don't go alone! I'll come with you."

"But we cannot continue this fight on the street. It has gone far enough. It is *over.* I simply cannot be hounded like this for something I have written, particularly by you. Darling, this is writing, that is all it is!"

"But published *as* it is—"

"Jesus Christ, *is* this Eastern fucking Europe? I will not be put in that position! That is *too* absurd! I won't have it! You cannot stop me from writing what I write for a simple and ridiculous pathological reason—because I cannot stop myself! I write what I write the way I write it, and if and when it should ever happen, I will publish what I publish however I want to publish and I'm not going to start worrying at this late date what people misunderstand or get wrong!"

"Or get right."

"We are talking about a notebook, a blue-print, a diagram, and not about human beings!"

"But you are a human being, whether you like it or not! And so am I! And so is she!"

"She's not, she's *words*—and try as I will, I cannot fuck words! I'm going out—alone!"

"HELLO? Hello?"

"Hello."

" . . . Hello."

"It's me."

"I know. I recognize your voice."

"I certainly recognize yours."

"How are you?"

"How am I? I'm okay. How are you? That's what I was calling about."

"I'm fine. I've been trying to call you. But I didn't know where to reach you. I tried your number. Your old number is not operative."

"In what country were you trying to call me?"

"Your studio in England."

"I'm not there anymore. I'm living in America for good now. Look, how are you?"

"I'm very well. I've been thinking so much about you. Ever since I read your book I haven't known whether to call or not. I thought about it a lot."

"I'll bet you did. I thought about it too. I thought about its effect on your marriage."

"Oh, well, he didn't read it."

Laughing. "Wonderful. Of course. All that worrying for nothing. How are you anyway? Tell me."

"I'm fine, aren't I? I don't know where to begin really."

"Did you wonder why I didn't call you?"

"No, I didn't. I just thought it was a decision. The last time we'd spoken, I don't think everybody was very happy. You made it very clear you had to go your way. I thought, yes, you have to go your way and I suppose I have to go mine. And that was a couple of years ago. So I went my way and you went yours."

"Yes."

"Well, I'm very glad you called because I've missed you such a lot. For a long time I didn't call because you said you didn't want to see me because it wasn't a love affair any longer. So I—"

"No, no. You said you didn't want to see *me*. You said you couldn't take any more of this guilty secret stuff."

"Did I?"

"Yes. Many times. You know I have a good memory."

"Goodness, do you! I was astonished. And in that way you betrayed yourself, because two people said, 'I heard you in that book.' To me."

"Really?"

"Yes, exactly my voice."

"Who said that?"

"I do have friends who read literature and who also listen to me."

"Well, you have a distinctive delivery. I was in love with you for twenty reasons but that was one of them. For me, it was a long, wonderful, finally very sad, important—"

"I would say the same."

"I don't think anyone's ever been quite so appreciated before. I was nuts about you."

"Oh."

"Did you know?"

"I . . . oh, dear. . . ."

"Don't turn English."

"Well, I was thinking . . ."

"You were thinking what?"

"Why it didn't happen. As it does in the book. One of the reasons was that you were away so much, particularly at the beginning. And it stayed in the world of fantasy. It stayed like a dream, really. It was so enclosed."

"You've been on my mind so much."

"Well, I've been thinking about you too."

"Shall I start the 'Remember that afternoon we' stuff?"

"Yes! Yes!" Laughing. "I'm not young anymore, by the way. When I met you I was still young. When you get to be thirty-eight it's suddenly all over. You know what I mean. It's not all all over but some of it's all over."

"The glow gone?"

"Oh, that was gone probably around the age of nineteen. I'll be thirty-nine any minute. I'm thinking of having a party in the dinosaur hall of the Natural History Museum."

"That's a lovely place. That's a very good idea."

"I just mean I think I'm turning that corner of thinking of myself quite differently. You know, when you absolutely don't think of yourself as a girl, you don't . . . I don't know, it's hard to put quickly, but that transition, which is so difficult for women, is one that I've begun. I'm sure you've heard about it."

"I didn't call before because I didn't want to disturb your life again. Are you still living together?"

"Yes. Are you?"

"Yes."

"We get on much better."

"Maybe I had something to do with it."

"Oh, I would think so. One of the reasons that I didn't call you again, though I didn't think I should anyway, was that I didn't realize that I was pregnant when I last saw you. I have another child."

"Oh, my. Do you?"

"Yes. And I find that's very ironic. Given the book. And of course it's a boy. So there we are. He's a very nice boy."

"Whose boy is it?"

"It's, it's my husband's . . . it is."

"Okay. I had to ask."

"He asked too."

"Are you sure? That it's his?"

"Absolutely certain."

"Well, ironies abound. You had the son all right but not by my character and not in my book. I imagined it but he did it. That's the difference between us; that's why you live with him and not me."

"Yes. That's life for you. Always slightly askew fiction."

"So you're the mother of two."

"Yup."

"You said that sadly."

"Ah well, I just think the phrase has some sad connotations. But they're lovely children. I've kind of been very busy these days counting my blessings."

"And so you and your husband are just hitting it off now?"

"Well, doing the decent thing, you know? I keep wondering where the big problem is these days. Obviously there are the intractable problems. Loneliness—I feel terribly lonely, I get quite bored sometimes at my job. But still, short of the big ones, there's nothing wrong."

"Do you have a lover?"

"No. No, I don't. Listen, I was astonished to see this character so terribly passive. I had simply no idea. Insofar as it's me . . ."

"Insofar as it's you, insofar, it's pretty much you."

"Well, I'm not like that anymore." Laughing. "I'm a positive person now."

"Are you, really? Thank God that happened after I wrote about you. Positive people in books put me to sleep."

"But the passivity—it was terrifying. To me that's a portrait of somebody who's in deep trouble. Somebody who's absolutely out of the ordinary swim of life. Don't you think?"

"Well, at a certain point the writing did take over and alter things."

"I can see where it came from, however. A friend of mine, just a few weeks ago, he'd finished the book and he asked me just how many times I'd had lunch with you. He said, 'There's a character in this book that's extraordinarily like you.' My husband was sitting right there. I said something noncommittal. I don't know what I said."

"You said, 'I don't eat lunch.' "

"I didn't really know how to say anything tremendously clever at that point. The other thing that troubled me is why, why do you *do* that? Why do you take life like that? And especially considering that you wanted secrecy—and our relationship was *distorted* by secrecy, by your almost paranoid efforts to keep the whole thing hidden. For the sake of your wife. Why did you then write a book which she, I'm sure, can't help but think is based on a real person? Why?"

"Because it's what I do. It wasn't paranoia. It was never paranoia. It was protecting somebody from something she couldn't be expected to be happy about. Besides, she thinks the real person is Rosalie Nichols."

"Oh, of course. Of yesteryear."

"Yes. Who did live upstairs like the woman in the book."

"Well, I know all that. We talked about her. She was at Oxford with me."

"I know."

"How funny. And what does Rosalie Nichols think?"

"It fooled her too. She said, 'All the time I thought you loved me for my body when in fact it was only for my sentences.'"

"I knew she would say that to you. I knew that would happen, I just knew she would think it was herself. She's having a fine time, I'll bet. And I also expect to be *told* by someone or other, sooner or later, that it's her."

"That'll be original, won't it?"

"Not only do you steal my words, you've given them to someone else."

"You want to be angry about that too?"

"I don't like it much."

"Would you have liked it better if I'd included in a footnote your name and address?"

"All of it's difficult. Angry, yes. I *was* angry. I thought if I was in your wife's position I'd know immediately that he'd been being consumed by somebody else for a very long time. And it seemed to me a complete reversal of everything you said. All the deformities imposed on our time together were pointless, because you'd done this anyway."

"Well, I wasn't worried about me—I had

Rosalie as my beard. I thought it was going to be worse for you."

"It could have been. In fact, who knows? It could well be in the future."

"And you have another child, which comes as—well, not a blow . . . but . . . well, a blow, yes. I did love you terribly."

"I think you may be idealizing me from afar. I'd think that by this time the reality would be unable to compare, if not with what you now remember, with what you wrote. The one you loved so terribly may not be unfictional little me."

"It was you. I couldn't have written about her that way if it hadn't been for you. I don't know if I ever told you how much or if I even knew how much *until* I wrote the book. There were certain necessary restraints all around. We had an awfully good time, even locked up in that terrible room. But I wasn't just living with you in those few hours —I had a life with you when I was writing. I had an imaginary life with you when you weren't there. It was all very strong."

"But you *can't*. You *can't* have an imaginary life and a real life simultaneously like that. And it was probably the imaginary life you had with me and the real life you had with her. Listen, you can't take down everything someone says like that."

"But I did. I do."

"Well, I felt quite angry about it. Rather like those native people who don't want their photographs taken; it takes something away from their souls."

"I'm sure you were angry."

"Very angry, yes."

"When did you get over it?"

"I probably haven't got over it."

"I've missed talking to you."

"And taking down what I say."

"Of course."

"But, you know . . . I've missed talking to *you*. I've missed talking to you so badly. I talk to you sometimes in my head."

"I talk to you too."

"I don't think Freshfield was at all a good name for me. You should have consulted me about that."

"It comes by way of an English poem. 'Tomorrow to fresh woods and pastures new.' "

"I realized that. But it wasn't all right. It was too easy."

"You haven't lost your bite."

"Our experience with the anti-Semitic woman in the restaurant—all the English reviewers said it was impossible in every detail."

"Yes." Laughing. "I thought you might come forward to defend me."

Laughing. "They thought it was too much a feat of imagination."

"Yes. They should go out to eat more often."

"So should we have."

"Well, we tried but that broad put us in our place. After that, I wasn't going out with you again, not in a Christian country I wasn't."

"Is that why you're living back in America? Is that why you've given up coming here—because the place is too Christian for you? That's what it sounds like from your book."

"My book's a book. I left for lots of reasons. Our parting was one."

"Yes, but in the novel it's England that I sort of stand for. Isn't it? I've been thinking about it. I sort of turned you into a foreigner here. Made you realize that England is not for you."

"Everything made me realize that. Did you turn me into a foreigner? I see what you're saying, but actually you cut both ways. Listening to you sometimes did make me feel an outsider but an outsider who, through you, was a little of an insider too. I learned from you. It isn't that you eluded me; it's that you made clear to me how much everything eluded me. Before I knew you I thought something of the place was getting through. But the more I knew you the more I felt as though I were spending half of each year in twelfth-century China. In the end I didn't understand anything."

"How could you expect to, all day hiding out in a little room without even a bed in it? Now that you're back, do you understand everything there?"

"I understand something. I take long walks in New York, and every once in a while I stop and find I'm smiling. I hear myself saying aloud, 'Home.' "

"So you're one of those people who careen around the New York streets talking to themselves. I've seen them there. I thought they were crazy."

"No, just all back from their service in England. Walking the streets I do see something I was missing terribly. Something I was longing for. It didn't occur to me, at least not in any blatant way, until I was back a few months."

"What's that?"

"Jews."

"We've got some of them in England, you know."

"Jews with force, I'm talking about. Jews with appetite. Jews without shame. Complaining Jews who get under your skin. Brash Jews who eat with their elbows on the table. Unaccommodating Jews, full of anger, insult, argument, and impudence. New York's the real obstreperous Zion, whether Ariel Sharon knows it or not."

"So England *was* too Christian for you."

"Tel Aviv's too Christian compared to this place. After London even Ed Koch looks good."

"Who's he?"

"The Jewish mayor my liberal friends hate. Not me. I watch him waving his arms on television, I hear that singsong, self-satisfied ethnic squawk, and I lean forward and kiss the set. The other day I was driving to Jersey to see my father, and coming out of the Lincoln Tunnel, the guy in the next car called me an asshole. He rolls down the window and he says, 'You fuckin' asshole, you!' I didn't even know what I'd done wrong. I just smiled. I told him, 'Force the issue, man. Pour it on.' All that truculence. All that wholehearted, unapologetic pugnacity—absolutely rejuvenating. When I see everybody everywhere pushing to be first, I begin to remember what it means to be human."

"So you've returned to the bosom of the tribe."

"Yes, I have. Isn't that odd?"

"Not very. The one who has gone home. You've read the *Odyssey*."

"I see. Another little epic of exile and return. With you as who? As Nausicaä? Calypso?"

"As Homer. I have been thinking about writing a book about *you*."

"Charge ahead."

"And do you know what it would be called? This is not the object of the enterprise. It's the very subject of the book. *Kiss and Tell*. Can you imagine how terrible this could be?"

"For whom?"

"For *you*."

"Do what you like."

"That's not the way I think. You know that I object greatly to writing down exactly what people said. I object greatly to this taking people's lives and putting them into fiction. And then being a famous author who resents critics for saying that he doesn't make things up."

"Because you had a baby doesn't mean I didn't make up a baby; because you're you doesn't mean I didn't make *you* up."

"I also exist."

"Also. You also exist and also I made you up. 'Also' is a good word to remember. You also don't exist as only you."

"I certainly don't anymore."

"You never did. As I made you up, you *never* existed."

"Then who was that in your studio with my legs over your shoulders? Please, no more of this highbrow nonsense. I'm English and I don't even hear it. What's wonderful about English culture is that we're either too damn sensible or too damn stupid to listen to that stuff. All I began to say is that I have very muddled, complex feelings about the whole business of self-exposure and the different kinds of betrayal, and what all these things amount to."

"Betrayal is an overpowering charge, don't

you think? There was no contract drawn up stating that in matters pertaining to you I would forswear my profession. I am a thief and a thief is not to be trusted."

"Not even by his moll?"

"However visible you may be feeling, you weren't identified in that book or made overly identifiable. However much you may have served as a model, the great British public happens to be ignorant of it and you only have not to tell them for them to remain ignorant."

"Don't bristle so. I didn't just say to you my feelings were simple about all this—I said they were complex. And they are. What it comes down to is that a woman comes to a man to chat a little, and all the man is really thinking about is his typewriter. You love your typewriter more than you could ever love any woman."

"I don't think that was so with you. I believe I loved you both equally."

"Well, I happen to know that whenever you feel agitated and ambivalent, then you do indeed have something to write about. And it—*my* book—is all about kissing and telling, because if I were to write this book I would be doing that. I haven't described it at all well to you."

"You have."

"Should I write it?"

"I'm not the one to say no, especially as I may do another about you."

"You wouldn't. You're not. You aren't, are you?"

Laughing. "Yes, of course I will. This'll be part of it."

"Well, I'd be amazed. I would call that scraping the barrel, really."

"Don't underestimate yourself. You're a great barrel. For me you were."

"Was I? Oh, I felt so angry. I was angry for months. Although I was very torn, really, because as soon as I read it, I also couldn't be angry."

"Why was that?"

"Because it was so, so tender . . . I think. Unless I got it wrong."

"No. I thought there were some things you'd like. Things I planted just for you to be amused by."

"Oh, there were. I didn't miss them. It was very strange reading it, absolutely strange. Because I was in no doubt which of it was addressed to me. I may have been wrong but I felt no doubt. And which bits of it were not, particularly."

"I'm sure you didn't miss any of it. But that was our life, I thought, as it might have been. Our life also."

"I saw. I saw. It's such a strange story."

"I know. No one would believe it."